Bad Times for Ghosts

Bad Times
for Ghosts

Bad Times
for Ghosts

W. J. M. Wippersberg

Designed and Illustrated by KÄTHI BHEND-ZAUGG
Translated by Edna McCown

HBJ

GULLIVER BOOKS
HARCOURT BRACE JOVANOVICH
San Diego   Austin   Orlando

Copyright © 1984 by Benziger Verlag Zürich, Köln and Obelisk Verlag
Innsbruck
English translation copyright © 1986 by Harcourt Brace Jovanovich, Inc.
Originally published in Switzerland as SCHLECHTE ZEITEN FÜR
GESPENSTER

Library of Congress Cataloging-in-Publication Data
Wippersberg, W. J. M. (Walter J. M.), 1945–
Bad times for ghosts.
Translation of: Schlechte Zeiten für Gespenster.
"Gulliver books."
Summary: Young Max Poltergeist and his ghost family fall on hard times
as they come to realize humans are no longer afraid of ghosts, but they
finally find a place for themselves in a Scottish castle in need of
haunting.
[1. Ghosts—Fiction] I. Bhend-Zaugg, Käthi, ill. II. Title.
PZ7.W7685Bad 1986   [Fic]   86-45058
ISBN 0-15-200413-0
ISBN 0-15-200414-9 (pbk.)

Printed in the United States of America
First United States edition
A B C D E

I had crawled back into the farthest, darkest corner of the dungeon, not quite giving up hope for a good fight.

My chances weren't bad: Papa was looking for Grandfather's head. Of course, he wasn't looking for it himself; he was standing there ordering everyone else to do it. But no one was paying attention to him, and he was quickly losing patience.

Mama was sitting before the mirror, plucking her eyebrows. Next, she would put on her makeup and spend a lot of time on her teeth and her hair. If Papa began making fun of her "silly face painting," as he called it, it was possible that she would start the fight.

Grandmama was wandering around somewhere out-

side in the dark. There's no way that she'll be back in time, I thought, and she won't want to change. That's sure to make Mama furious.

Lily was busy with her poisonous spiders. If *I* wanted to pick a fight, all I had to do was say something about the spiders and Lily would start screaming. Mama usually came to my rescue, but Papa would take Lily's side, and that always held the promise of a good family argument.

But I didn't need to interfere yet because the atmosphere was already tense enough.

"I need help finding Grandfather's head!" Papa said for at least the twentieth time. "It couldn't have just disappeared!"

"I can't say that I care," Mama murmured. She was rummaging through a drawer. "I'm more interested in finding out where my tooth file is."

"Grandfather can't go out without his head. How would that look?" Papa snarled. "If we don't find his head, we're all staying home!"

That's exactly what I wanted—to stay at home. But

3

for that to happen, everybody would first have to start screaming at once. Then, after catching a glimpse of herself in the mirror, Mama would start to cry and say that it was "imposssible" for her to leave the house looking the way she did.

"My tooth file! Where is my tooth file? It must be here somewhere!" Mama muttered, still rummaging in her drawer. Then she shrieked, "Who has taken my file again?"

"Max, naturally," Lily answered. "I saw him filing his fingernails with it."

That was true, but I still came out of my corner and kicked her in the shins. I kicked her so hard that she started shrieking, too.

I had hoped that our quarreling would fuel Mama's anger, but she only looked at us for a moment and sighed. "Imposssible! You two are simply imposssssible! Why must you always carry on this way?"

Papa, who was usually proud of Lily's piercing scream, covered his ears and shouted as loud as he could, "You

all will help me look for Grandfather's head right away, or I'll—"

"Or you'll what?" Mama asked. "Grandfather is old enough to take care of his own head. He should have learned that much in eight hundred years."

She didn't seem as interested in fighting as she did in making herself beautiful. Pulling up her top lip, Mama looked in the mirror and moaned, "It's impossssible for me to go out with such dull teeth. Lilofee will tell everyone that they're dull."

"And Dragul will laugh himself silly if Grandfather arrives without his head!" Papa replied.

"He probably forgot it yesterday at the tavern," Lily said. Then she tried to talk us all into helping her catch flies. "I need a few more flies. My poor spiders will starve if I'm gone all night."

"They should catch their own flies, the fat things," Papa growled. It was a good sign when Papa insulted Lily's spiders because it meant he was in a foul mood.

I waited for Lily to scream again, but she didn't.

Lily's Poisonous Spiders

8 legs
8 tiny eyes
2 jointed poisonous fangs

Copied from Lily's natural science book (the chapter entitled "Pets for Ghosts")

The garden spider is a particularly suitable pet for young ghosts. It weaves a wonderful web every night.

The garden spider is simple to care for. It needs nothing more than a live fly and a little water each day. Drop the water onto the web with a wet toothbrush.

To catch a garden spider, lure it out of its hiding place with a tuning fork. Strike the tuning fork, and hold it against the web. The spider will feel the vibration and come out to catch the "insect."

Hold a jar under the spider, and tease it with a twig. It will fall off into the jar!

Housefly (enlarged)

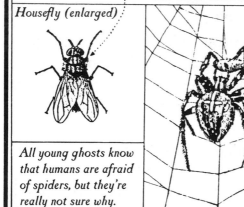

All young ghosts know that humans are afraid of spiders, but they're really not sure why.

Garden spider embalming a fly

This garden spider cage is constructed from a box with a black background and glass or Plexiglas front. Remember the air holes! For wooden frame cages, staple on black material as a background.

The garden spider spins two types of thread: smooth suspension threads (S) and sticky threads for trapping insects. This illustration shows the spider weaving the sticky threads from the outside in. After their webs are completed, spiders then eat their support spirals (H).

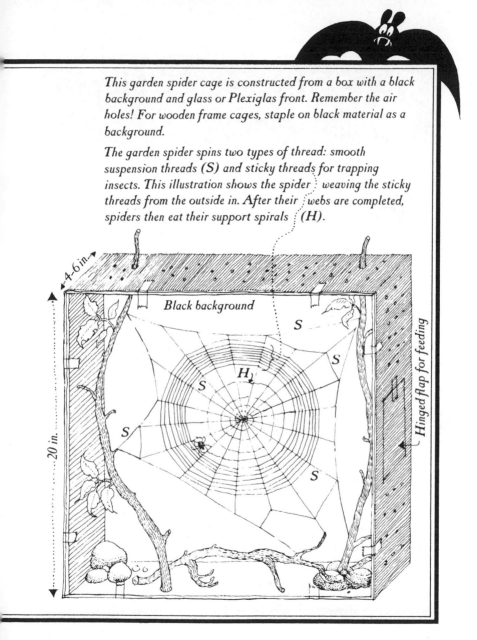

4-6 in.

20 in.

Black background

Hinged flap for feeding

S

S

S

H

S

S

Instead, she was sitting very still, as though she were listening to something. I listened, too. And sure enough, I heard a faint buzzing. We both watched as a fly circled Mama's head and landed on her mirror.

Lily crouched and sprang. She actually caught the fly, although in doing so, she knocked over one of Mama's pots of white makeup. That was when Mama really screamed.

And then—I couldn't have wished for anything better—Papa started to roar that he'd had enough. E N O U G H E N O U G H E N O U G H. Entirely enough. "You're all driving me crazy!" he yelled. He swore he would N E V E R N E V E R N E V E R go through that again. . . .

Meanwhile, Grandfather had been standing there the whole time, unobserved. Since he didn't have his head, he could ask for help only by moving his arms. From time to time he would point where ears are usually found, as if to say, "Listen, please, somebody!" And finally, when Mama stopped screaming and Papa stopped bellowing, we could indeed hear his voice.

"If you had really wanted to look for me," it said crossly, "instead of raising the dead, you could have found me a long time ago."

"Under the bed!" Lily cried, and went to get a broom. Then, kneeling beside the bed, she began to poke around.

"Kindly watch out for my ears!" the voice scolded. "And—ouch—my nose, too!" But Lily had already fished the head out.

"The file is under there, too," the head said as Papa carried it over to Grandfather, who tucked it under his arm, where it belonged.

Mama ordered Lily to retrieve the file as well and immediately began sharpening her upper eyeteeth with it.

Papa watched her for a while, impatiently drumming his fingers on the table. When he'd had enough of that, he decided to pay a visit to the refrigerator.

"Our dear relatives will certainly serve blood sausage again—always blood sausage," he said, finishing off the baked bat ears left over from lunch the night before.

"Where is Grandmama floating around?" Grandfather asked.

"Outside, as usual," answered Lily, who had again taken up her search for flies. "She's floating over the fields, trying to glow. I think she believes she's a will-o'-the-wisp today." The tone of Lily's voice made it clear that she thought Grandmama was a little crazy. I hoped that Papa would scold her and get the argument, which had died down, going again.

But Papa only muttered, "Don't talk about your grandmother like that." He was still chewing on the bat ears, though, and some of it fell out of his mouth, leaving a spot on the freshly starched dress shirt he was wearing. Unfortunately Mama didn't notice; otherwise she would have really let him have it.

I thought about drawing her attention to it, but by then she was already calling to me, "Max! Bring Grandmama in here right away! I'm sure she hasn't changed and will want to go out in her work smock again."

So I got up, slipped through the narrow door of the dungeon, and glided up the damp, moldy steps. *I can*

still recall that delicious smell, and it brings back strong memories of our wonderful old apartment even today.

I paused under the castle gate. It was pleasantly cool outside. The pale full moon was half-hidden by clouds. Under the castle's cliffs a light fog rose from the earth. Bats darted by. Somewhere an owl hooted, and the sky looked as though there would be a storm during the night. *I almost get homesick when I think back on it all.*

The only things that disturbed the perfect setting were the crane that towered over the castle and the construction equipment that stood in the courtyard. They made so much noise during the day that I couldn't sleep. *Only now, more than a year later, do I realize that we couldn't have stayed in the castle much longer—even if what began on that evening hadn't begun. Humankind's iron machinery in the courtyard should have been a warning to us. But we did our best not to pay*

11

attention to it, and the grown-ups acted as though we were invulnerable to the modernization going on around us.

On that particular evening I just turned my back. I didn't want to see the machines.

"Grandmamaaaa!" I called. "Boooo, Graaaandmama! It's time to come in now!"

There was no answer. But I saw a shadow gliding between the trees in the orchard, and soon afterward Grandmama was standing beside me.

"Did you see me glowing?" she asked.

I could only shake my head. "You don't glow, not even a bit. You're not a will-o'-the-wisp. Besides, there's no such thing anymore. They've died out because there are no moors left for them to light up." We had learned that in school.

"Yes, yes." Grandmama sighed. "Everything is different today; today everything is different."

Just as we were entering the dungeon, Mama discovered the grease spot on Papa's shirt.

"Imposssssible, you are not leaving the castle looking

like that!" she shrieked, and bared her needle-sharp, well-filed eyeteeth so threateningly that I began to again have hope for a fight.

"What will Dragul and Lilofee think of us if you show up in a soiled shirt?" Mama shouted. If Papa had gotten stubborn about it, then the fight might have broken out in full force, and it's possible that I would have been spared the visit to our relatives—and the journey there, which at that time was something I feared more than anything else. The path we had to take led past a hideous village that was inhabited by humans.

But Papa didn't get stubborn. He did carry on about how he couldn't stand Dragul and Lilofee, that consequently he couldn't care less what they thought of him, and that he had had ENOUGH ENOUGH ENOUGH of the pretentious way they carried on. He also declared that he had no desire to visit them, not today, not tomorrow, NEVER NEVER NEVER. But then he went to put on a fresh shirt.

It was more difficult for Mama to convince Grandmama that she could not possssibly go out in her work

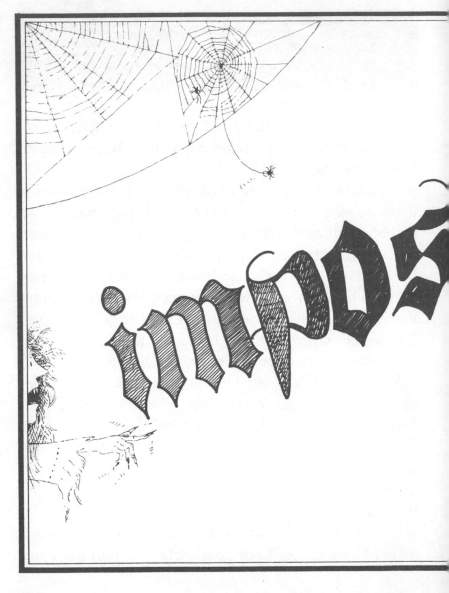

Paint black!

ssible

15

smock. But after that had been settled, there was nothing more to delay our departure.

We were about to leave when Lily pointed out that Grandfather had misplaced his head again. This time we all searched, and much to my disappointment, the head was quickly found.

"I suppose we're all ready now," Papa said. "If it's necessary to go at all, then let's go now."

"I wonder if it's like this when other families go out together," Mama said thoughtfully while she closed the iron gate to the dungeon.

As we crossed the castle courtyard, Lily said, "Maybe we'll meet some humans. I'll screech so loud that they'll lose their hearing and eyesight." But just then she stumbled over a shovel and fell flat on her face.

"These people just let things fall where they may, fall where they may," Grandmama fussed.

I simply could not understand, *not at that time anyway*, how the others could talk so matter-of-factly, so indifferently about humans, those strange and horrible creatures whose faces were said to be frightfully rosy

and in some cases absolutely red. I had never seen a real person, but they showed us pictures of them in school—pictures so ghastly that I had daymares about them. Whenever I heard noises made by the construction machinery in the courtyard, the thought that one of them might suddenly appear by my bed nearly scared me to death.

What I really couldn't understand, *and still do not to this day*, was the bright lights people are so fond of. Not only do they go out during the light of day, but at night they also surround themselves with artificial light.

The village that we had to pass by on the way to Uncle Dragul's and Aunt Lilofee's castle was bathed in their weird night-light. I immediately shut my eyes when I saw its first pale reflection between the trees. I held tightly to Mama's hand. My heartbeat was so loud that I was sure everyone could hear it.

I was afraid that Papa was going to lecture me, as he often did when I behaved in that manner, but he was strangely silent. The thought that he might have

finally given up trying to make a properly gruesome ghost of me crossed my mind. But after we had traveled some distance, I heard him mutter:

"You can open your eyes now, Max, you little baby. We passed the village a long time ago, and you certainly won't meet any people out here."

19

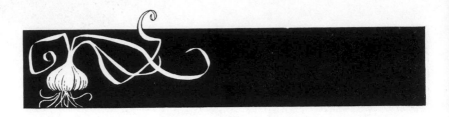

Uncle Dragul was in full evening dress as usual: black pants, a jet black coat with two tails in back, a snow-white shirt, and a bloodred vest.

"You're finally here!" he called, and bared his long vampire teeth, as though he wanted to greet us with a bite.

Little Alfred was dressed exactly like his father.

Aunt Lilofee wore a long white dress embroidered with a thousand silver bats.

Mathilda's white dress had only five hundred silver bats, but after all, she was much smaller than her mother.

Whenever I hadn't seen my dear relatives for a while, I found their habit of dressing like humans—as they did on that evening—truly spooky. That's why I would have preferred to skip the welcome, but Aunt Lilofee had already grabbed me and given me three kisses on my left cheek and three kisses on my right cheek. Uncle Dragul was satisfied patting my head.

Mathilda cut the welcome short by immediately telling Lily and me about her pile of new toys. "Your parents could never afford such expensive toys," she concluded.

"Don't say that!" Aunt Lilofee scolded her. "That is very rude. Anyway, what something costs doesn't matter."

"Of course it matters." Mathilda contradicted her. I decided on the spot that after dinner, when the grown-ups weren't looking, I was going to beat her up.

Then I thought: Why shouldn't I annoy Aunt Lilofee and Uncle Dragul a little right now? So I pulled little Alfred aside, grabbed his upper lip before he could defend himself, and said, "Still no eyeteeth, eh? You'll probably never make a good vampire!"

I saw his parents shudder. Their greatest fear was that their son looked more like a human child than he did the offspring of an age-old family of bloodsuckers. But not to be outdone, Alfred said, "You probably still get scared to death when you see a human." And then *my* parents shuddered.

"You children shouldn't be arguing already," Aunt Lilofee said with a forced laugh.

"That's right," Papa grumbled. "It would be better if you waited until after dinner to fight."

Since it was time for dinner, Uncle Dragul led the way into the castle's large dining hall.

Mama and Grandmama admired the silverware on the long table, just as Aunt Lilofee expected them to. Then we all were seated.

Grandfather put his head down in front of him and said, "A little something to drink before dinner wouldn't hurt, would it?"

Uncle Dragul immediately rang a tiny silver bell, and Otto appeared. He bowed and said in a mechanical voice, "I am at your service, Count. What is it that you wish?"

"Bring us a bottle of Scotch whisky and a couple of glasses," Uncle Dragul ordered, "and then you may serve dinner."

"Very well, Count. As you wish, Count," Otto rat-

tled, and he shuffled out the door, accompanied by the sound of squeaking joints.

"I have to oil him again," Uncle Dragul said.

"Isn't it time for his checkup?" Aunt Lilofee reminded him.

Of everyone and everything in the castle, Otto was my favorite, even if he did look almost like the humans in the pictures I'd seen in school. But only a bit, because Otto was not even three feet tall and his body parts didn't fit together too well. Uncle Dragul had had him made in a famous Transylvanian workshop. "He was very inexpensive," Aunt Lilofee liked to say, "because he didn't turn out to be very good-looking."

That was true. In fact, Otto's body looked like a barrel. His face was green, and his arms were a little short. But his hands were so big that when he returned to the dining hall, he was able to carry in his palms, without even using a tray, not only the whisky bottle and glasses but also the bowls of food. Grandfather immediately picked up the bottle, and carefully lifted

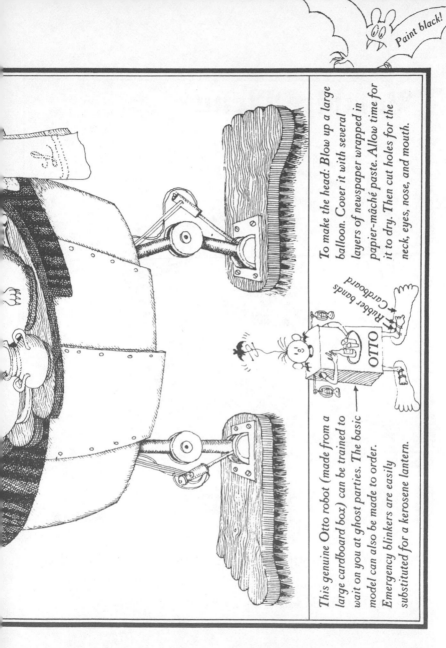

Paint black!

To make the head: Blow up a large balloon. Cover it with several layers of newspaper wrapped in papier-mâché paste. Allow time for it to dry. Then cut holes for the neck, eyes, nose, and mouth.

Rubber bands
Cardboard
OTTO

This genuine Otto robot (made from a large cardboard box) can be trained to wait on you at ghost parties. The basic model can also be made to order. Emergency blinkers are easily substituted for a kerosene lantern.

his head in his left hand. With his right, he put the bottle to his mouth, making sure not to spill a drop.

"That's great stuff, isn't it?" Uncle Dragul asked. "We brought it back with us from our vacation."

As Papa predicted, blood sausage was served as an

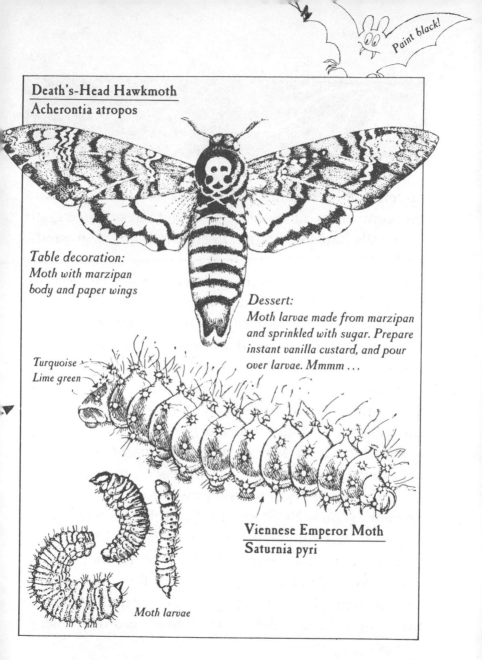

Paint black!

Death's-Head Hawkmoth
Acherontia atropos

Table decoration:
Moth with marzipan
body and paper wings

Dessert:
Moth larvae made from marzipan
and sprinkled with sugar. Prepare
instant vanilla custard, and pour
over larvae. Mmmm ...

Turquoise
Lime green

Viennese Emperor Moth
Saturnia pyri

Moth larvae

appetizer. Then came pickled leeches and a salad of different kinds of nightshade vegetables. For dessert we finally had something I liked: moth larvae in vanilla custard.

Outside, *I remember it as if it were yesterday*, a storm was brewing. Through the high windows I could see the clouds racing past the moon. Curtains fluttered. The candles smoked and flickered, throwing familiar ghostly shadows on the wall. Doors creaked and slammed in the castle and were blown open again by the storm. It could have been so nice and cozy if only the grown-ups hadn't spoiled it.

I couldn't have known at that moment what a far-reaching effect that night was to have on all our lives.

I only half listened to the grown-ups, but even with one ear I soon understood that our relatives had invited us just so they could talk about their vacation to England and Scotland, or more specifically, to brag about it.

For years, Aunt Lilofee explained, they had gone to Transylvania, Uncle Dragul's home. And although the moon over the Carpathian Mountains and the howling

of the wolves were certainly lovely, it did eventually get a little tiresome. "In England one meets many more interesting people," she said pretentiously. "The ghosts there almost all belong to the aristocracy, faaabulous people, who know how to give faaabulous parties."

"Oh, really?" Papa said. "My brother Percy isn't an aristocrat, but he's made it to the position of royal castle ghost. Anyway, he wrote that the English are deadly bores."

"But he also wrote that they have proper respect for ghosts," Mama said, and she told us about the letter in which Uncle Percy had invited us all to England for a visit.

None of us knew then just how soon we would have to accept his invitation.

The first big fight started earlier than usual that evening. Irritated by our relatives' bragging, Papa made fun of spooks who were willing to sleep in strange, uncomfortable beds and who suffered through totally unappetizing food in foreign countries, just so they could boast about it later. Uncle Dragul, Aunt Lilofee,

and Mama argued with him. And this time even Grandfather, who was always on Papa's side, disagreed with him. Grandfather announced that he could give only the highest praise to England and Scotland because any countries that could brew such excellent beverages must simply be wonderful. Then he poured his head another sip of whisky.

Grandmama tried again and again to make herself heard. "How I traveled in my youth; I traveled quite a lot," she said a few times, but no one paid attention because they all were talking at once and listening only to themselves. We children ate in silence. I grinned at Alfred and made two long eyeteeth with my fingers, just to tease him. I was sorry the table was so large; otherwise I could have kicked Mathilda, who was sitting across from me.
We had to wait until dinner was over and Uncle Dragul finally "rose from the table," as he put it, before we

were excused. As usual, the grown-ups were invited into the library for coffee.

"Or would you rather have tea?" Aunt Lilofee asked. "We brought some faaabulous tea back with us from England."

"I'll stick with whisky," Grandfather said, taking his head under his right arm and the bottle under his left.

"You children may go play now," said Aunt Lilofee, who didn't notice that we were already on our way.

The playroom was almost as big as the dining hall, but much nicer because it was lit by a single torch.

Mathilda showed us her new werewolf doll that howled when she pushed on its stomach.

"This kind of doll is terribly expensive," Mathilda said. "Your parents couldn't afford it. But it's not your fault that you have a common poltergeist for a father."

"That's right," Alfred added, "not everyone can come from a very old, aristocratic family."

"Our mother," Lily stated, "is your father's sister,

Werewolf Dolls

Send away for our
current price list!

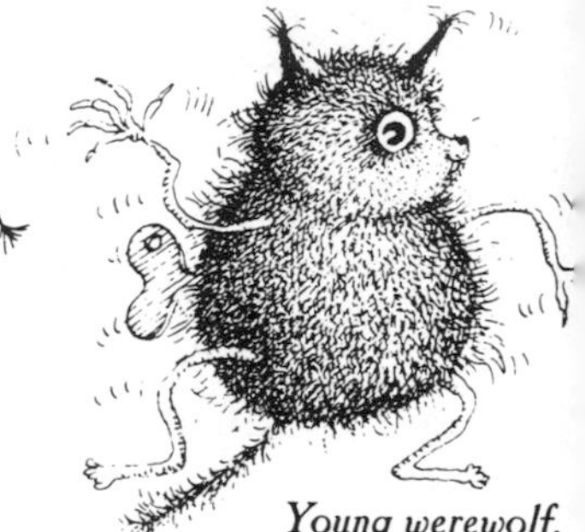

Werewolf

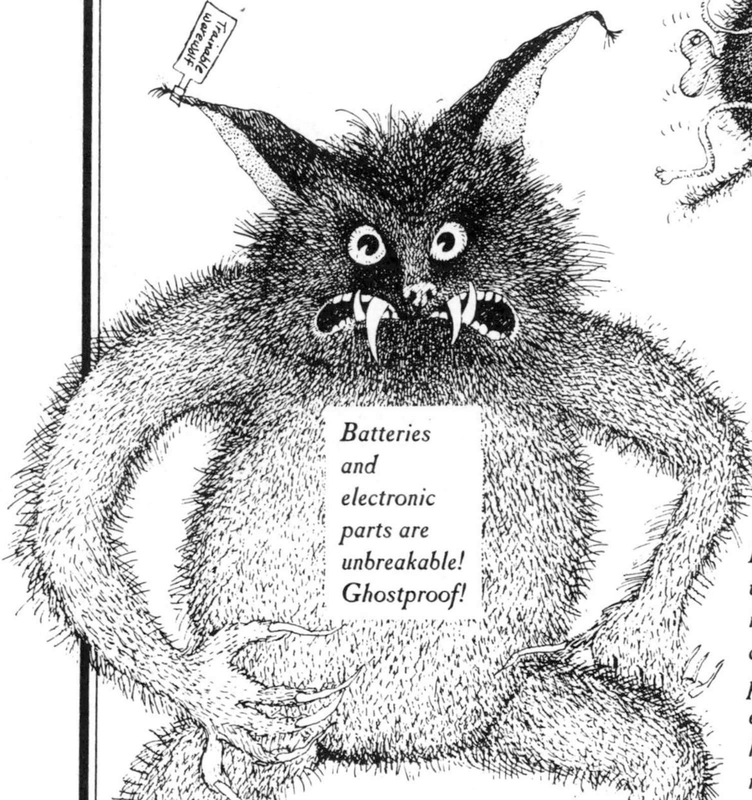

*Batteries
and
electronic
parts are
unbreakable!
Ghostproof!*

*Young werewolf.
Our most popular
model comes in
angora for your
little ones. Once
wound, it's
guaranteed to dance
for thirty-four
seconds.*

*Large fighting
werewolf (thirty-six
inches). This model
comes with movable
parts, blinking green
eyes, and a realistic
howl. The easy-care
nylon can be brushed
or combed (use carpet
shampoo).*

32

Inflatable model
for the bath
(supply limited)!

Transylvanian gray wolf
with real rabbit fur.
This one likes to
snuggle and bite!

*Little Spook
Quality Toy®*

Knitted werewolf
mask and gloves.
The fur is genuine
steel wool.

Delivered by owl to your home!

33

so we come from the exact same family that you do." Lily spoke quietly. Then she let out such a sudden scream that Mathilda seemed momentarily paralyzed. Lily used the opportunity to box her ears.

What I had been waiting for since our arrival finally happened: Mathilda began to howl. Alfred wanted revenge and grabbed Lily by the hair. By then I had caught him by the tails of his silly dinner costume, and the four of us ended up rolling around on the floor, slugging each other.

When we got tired, we unknotted ourselves. "That wasn't a bad start," Alfred said contentedly. "But now what are we going to do?"

"We could play 'Catch the Hat or Don't Get Angry,' " I suggested.

We all liked that game, so everyone agreed. But when Mathilda was caught cheating, the fight started all over again. Lily screamed louder than before, and Alfred howled like a wolf. Mathilda howled, too—from pain because I was pulling her hair with both hands.

I could just imagine what the grown-ups were talking about in the library. They must have heard our yelling and screaming, and Grandmama had surely said, "How nice that the children are enjoying themselves." And probably: "My goodness, what fun I had when I was young; my goodness, what fun I had."

While we were busy beating each other up, Papa no doubt talked about what a bad time it was for ghosts.

Grandfather probably went on about the Thirty Years War and how he had caused fear and uncertainty in both the Swedish and German armies. *All the great moments in ghost history took place decades, even centuries, ago. It's amazing that our recent lack of achievement wasn't obvious to me before now.*

Mama and Aunt Lilofee certainly must have chatted about the newest ghost fashions they had seen in the latest style magazines.

There was no question in my mind that Papa and Uncle Dragul were disagreeing about something. After all, they disagreed about almost everything.

But it wasn't until we were on our way home that evening that I found out what they had fought about while Lily, Mathilda, Alfred, and I were innocently crashing about—and what the consequences of that fight were.

It was shortly before dawn when we finally made our way home, and I was afraid that day would break before we reached the castle.

I somehow figured out that Papa and Uncle Dragul had made a bet between them. It also became clear that Mama didn't approve of it; she found the whole thing imposssssible. But what I couldn't quite understand from her whispered accusations was what it was all about. When I asked her directly, she would only say that I didn't need to worry, that she would talk Papa out of it. *I should have guessed then that their bet had something to do with me, but I didn't.*

Papa was in a great mood. He only laughed at

Mama's displeasure. He'd had a few too many whiskies and was floating a little aboveground because he couldn't walk straight.

"Hee-hee-hee," he laughed again and again, sounding more like a goat than a ghost. "I really gave it to him tonight, didn't I? He's deserved it for a long time, the old braggart!"

"You're an old braggart yourself," Mama replied. But she couldn't say anything to spoil Papa's mood.

My grandparents were behind us, so I waited for them, hoping that Grandmama would tell me what was going on. But she avoided my question and said, "I'll have nothing to do with it. Your father will soon see what comes of all this, he'll see."

It didn't make sense to ask Grandfather. He was too caught up in his memories of the best years of his male life (as he calls them). He walked at a brisk pace, and from under his arm, his head bawled one of the songs commonly sung by soldiers during the Thirty Years War.

Lily also had no idea what was going on, although

she heard something about Papa betting on his ghost's honor and Uncle Dragul on his vampire's honor. That sounded serious. They'd often bet on a few bottles of schnapps, but never on their honor.

Papa repeated again and again the things he had said to Uncle Dragul, things that he was proud of. "He looked so very stupid, good old Dragul, when I told him . . ." he would begin to say. Or, "He really didn't expect that I . . ." But each time Mama kept him from finishing his sentence.

Papa didn't appreciate her interruptions and quickly put an end to them. "Everyone knows that travel is educational. In order to get a proper education, children must see the world," he said, and it was clear that he was imitating Uncle Dragul. His laugh echoed through the early-morning darkness. "You can't expect me to listen to that without saying something," he said in his own voice. "And you can't disagree with what I said. They can travel all over the world with their little Alfred, but they will NEVER NEVER NEVER make a real vampire out of him. That hit home, didn't it? Old

Dragul never expected me to say that to his face."

Papa wasn't able to contain himself much longer, and five minutes later I found out exactly what was going on. Because he had been making fun of Alfred, Uncle Dragul began to make fun of me. According to him I wasn't a terribly impressive ghost. And he didn't believe that someone who was afraid of people could ever be successful in scaring them. They both continued on like that until Papa bet Uncle Dragul that within a few weeks he could make me into a ghost capable of scaring people to death whenever I wished. At first they bet their usual bottle of schnapps, the kind that Papa says smells very much like sulfur and brimstone and causes his throat to burn  deliciously. But then he raised the bet, crying, "No, this time we bet on our honor, my ghost's against your vampire's!" *To this day, I'm still not sure I know what he meant by that, but anyway they both agreed.*

Naturally I was shocked. The thought that Papa might actually drag me in front of a creepy human—as he often threatened to do—and instruct me to grind my teeth, roll my eyes, and wail "boo!" and "aagh!" was worse than any punishment I could imagine. Mama whispered a promise that she would talk Papa out of it, and I clung to the hope that she could.

At that time it didn't occur to me to question her promise, even though she and Grandmama complained about my unghostly tendencies more than Papa did. The funny thing is, no one in the family had ever taken the time to teach me how to be frightening.

We came to the village we'd passed on the way— the village that I was expected to terrorize. Trying not to let my fear show, I looked toward the east for signs of the dawning day.

When we finally reached our castle, Grandmama pointed out that Grandfather had somehow lost his head.

"He still had it near the village," Mama said with annoyance.

"And I heard him singing after that," Lily said.

Then Grandmama remembered that the singing had become softer and softer as we neared the castle. Grandfather, she decided, had dropped his head and had simply gone on without it.

We had no choice but to turn back and look for the head. It finally turned up in a gutter, asleep and snoring, but the search cost us a lot of time. I was so afraid that the terrible light of day would catch us by surprise that I couldn't stop the keys around my neck from shaking. *But compared to what the coming nights held in store for me, that was nothing.*

45

When I finally went to bed that morning, I was so exhausted by fear that I fell right to sleep. It was no small wonder that I was tormented by bad dreams. But early in the morning I was awakened by the construction equipment in the courtyard. It seemed to be louder than ever that day. I repeated to myself a hundred times that there was no reason to be afraid of humans. After all, a glimmer of the sun's early rays had caught us as we completed the last leg of our journey, and it hadn't been as bad as I expected. Still, I wasn't succeeding in talking myself out of being afraid. If you're afraid, you're afraid, and that's all there is to it. *At least that's how I felt about it then.*

I tossed and turned most of the day. When it was

time to get up that evening, I tried to convince myself that the bet had been only a part of my bad dreams. And as long as the subject wasn't brought up, I was almost able to believe it.

Lily had gotten up before me. I came across her crouched in a corner, scribbling in a notebook, the way she always did her homework at the last minute. I thought about asking her to help me come up with a way to escape Papa's plans for me. But devious as she was, I then thought the better of it and decided to find Grandfather instead.

Although Grandfather sometimes worried me with his talk about the bad times facing ghosts, I was still sure that he could help me. I crept over to my grandparents' room and found that Grandmama was already up.

Floating over to the bed, I pulled on the arm of Grandfather's nightshirt. His body woke up, but his head was nowhere to be seen. Grandfather reached over to the night table, found a pencil, and scribbled on a piece of paper: "I'M SORRY! YOUR GRAND-MOTHER HID MY HEAD DURING THE NIGHT."

"I put it outside," I heard Grandmama say. She had, as was her custom, come in quietly and was reading Grandfather's note over my shoulder. "That head snored so loud that I couldn't get any rest, no rest at all." She then shrieked, "Get up, you lazybones! It's already pitch-dark outside, pitch-dark already. Get out from under those sheets!"

"You know that he can't hear you if he doesn't have his head," I said to Grandmama.

"Oh, yes, right," Grandmama said and she followed me into the part of our apartment we called the living-dungeon.

Papa had been awakened by her shriek. The bumping, moaning, and rumbling that came from my parents' room made me shudder because I knew it meant that I'd have to face Papa before too long.

Lily heard the noise, too, because she slammed her notebook shut and ran into the bathroom just as Papa appeared in the doorway.

"Good evening!" I said as pleasantly as I could.

But Papa put his hands over his ears and said, "Not

so loud!" He didn't need to say anything about his headache—I knew he had one just by looking at him.

"He who can't hold his whisky shouldn't drink it; he who can't, shouldn't," Grandmama said in a very, very loud voice.

Papa shuddered in pain and stumbled in the direction of the bathroom. When he rattled the locked door, Lily called out, "I'm almost fi-i-nished!" I could tell Papa felt terrible because even that didn't make him angry the way it normally did when he wasn't able to get into the bathroom.

"My poor, poor head," he muttered as he sat down at the table. Turning to Grandmama, he asked, "How's Grandfather? If I remember correctly, he drank quite a bit himself last night."

"But unlike you, he knows his limits," Grandmama said. "Have you seen him drunk in the last three or four hundred years?"

I spoke up carefully. "But Grandfather's snoring was keeping Grandmama awake, so she put his head outside."

"I put it in the courtyard," she admitted.

"Grandfather's head was outdoors all day?" Papa asked in disbelief.

"I put an old bucket over it so the sun wouldn't do it any harm," Grandmama told us.

"But what would we have done if the construction workers had discovered it? Did you bother to think about that?" Papa asked, appearing to forget

his headache for the time being. "What would have happened if they had found Grandfather's head! Imagine what they would have done with it! You know how disrespectful people are these days!"

"Oh, really!" Grandmama said. Then she changed the subject and told us about the conversation she had with our neighbor, Mrs. Bag. "She maintains," Grandmama reported, "that the people are planning to turn our castle into a hotel and that our dungeon is to be a wine cellar." I wanted to ask them what would happen

to us if that happened, but just then Mama called us to breakfast (ghosts call it breakfast, too, although we eat it at night rather than in the morning). She greeted Grandmama and me with a smile and completely ignored Papa.

The bathroom door opened, and Lily finally came out. Before Papa could get up, though, I had already slipped in. As I shut the door, I heard him complaining about being late for work and how his employer, the head poltergeist, would be cross with him.

Then it was quiet. Even though I wasn't in the room, I knew that a tense, nervous silence had settled into the apartment, the kind that occurred whenever Papa had a headache and Mama was angry with him because of his reasons for having one.

So far nobody had said one word about the bet. And no one brought it up at breakfast either. Only after Papa excused himself and went to get dressed did Mama follow him with the intent of discussing the subject.

"You will go to see Dragul after work and tell him

that you got carried away last night," she said. "You both had far too much to drink, so the bet doesn't count."

"And how it counts!" Papa muttered as loud as he could without hurting his head. "If I withdraw the bet now, everyone will say that I don't have confidence in my son."

I was doing my best to hear their conversation, and Papa's last comment didn't escape my enlarged ears. (Ghosts are like that: If we especially want to hear something, our ears actually grow.)

For a split second his statement made me very happy. But then the full meaning of his words began to sink in.

"Do you know what could happen if something went wrong?" Mama asked.

"Nothing will go wrong," Papa said firmly. "Max," he said as he came into the room, "tonight, right after the midnight meal, we begin—I'm taking charge of your education. I'll arrange for the aftermidnight off of work and you're going to learn what being a

ghost is all about, once and for all. I'll make you the most frightening ghost that anyone has ever seen or heard. . . ."

Mama looked as if she had something to say, but Papa saw it coming. "I don't want to hear one word. You won't talk me out of it. Do *you* like knowing that everyone makes fun of our son?"

Mama turned to me and said, "Why do you have to make it so obvious that you're afraid of people?"

I didn't quite understand what she meant. "You can't hide something like that," I answered. "I've been the same since the first time I tried to scare someone."

Mama only shook her head. *And at that time—a year ago—I couldn't begin to understand what was on her mind.*

Like every other school night, the children next door, little Blubber Bag and little Pudge Bag, were waiting for Lily and me in the courtyard.

On the way to school they told us about their weekend outing. They had visited a city more than a ghost-hour away by air and had sneaked into the haunted

Bats

The brown long-eared bat (and all horseshoe-nosed bats) send ultrasonic waves through their noses.

The large mouse-eared bat sends ultrasonic waves through its open mouth, like most bats of the smooth-nosed variety.

Mouse-eared bat's wingspan

Bat radar doesn't work on ghosts; bats fly right through them!

Their ultrasonic waves bounce off solid beings (people, for example), so bats *NEVER* collide with them! Why, then, are people so afraid of them? If you have an answer to this question, please send it in to **Research** for **Young Ghosts** *Magazine*.

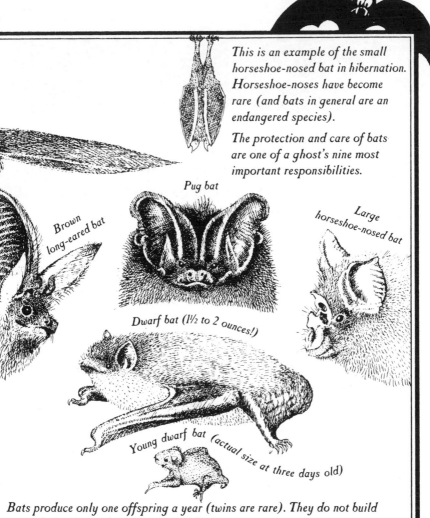

This is an example of the small horseshoe-nosed bat in hibernation. Horseshoe-noses have become rare (and bats in general are an endangered species).

The protection and care of bats are one of a ghost's nine most important responsibilities.

Pug bat

Brown long-eared bat

Large horseshoe-nosed bat

Dwarf bat (1½ to 2 ounces!)

Young dwarf bat (actual size at three days old)

Bats produce only one offspring a year (twins are rare). They do not build nests. At birth an infant bat is naked. It instinctively uses its claws to cling to its mother. A newborn is nursed during the day and is kept safe in a crowd of other bats at night, while its mother hunts. A mother is able to pick out her young from a group of several hundred bats.

house at an amusement park with their parents, Scream
Bag and Babble Bag. But strangely enough, the humans
had been more afraid of the ghosts made of cardboard,
plastic, and cloth than they had of the real thing.

I was only half listening to them because I couldn't
stop thinking about what was facing me at midnight. . . .

During my early evening classes I tried to think up
a way to get out of it. I even considered running away
from home. It was becoming more and more clear to
me that I just didn't want to be what my parents and
Grandmama called a "proper ghost." The truth was
that I had *never* wanted to be one! Up until that time
I hadn't given much thought to the notion that it was
a ghost's responsibility to frighten people. The whole
idea seemed silly to me. After all, I knew only too well
how horrible it was to be afraid. . . .

"Scaring people is silly!" I said to myself in the middle of history class. It came out a little too loud, I guess,
because the teacher, who was talking about some of

history's most famous ghosts stopped in mid-sentence.

"I can't believe my ears!" he cried. "Did I hear you correctly?"

It took a lot of hard work to convince the teacher that he had heard wrong. "What I said was that being scared is silly," I asserted for so long and with such conviction that he finally believed me.

I thanked my lucky stars that I had been able to get myself out of a very tight spot. Otherwise the consequences would have been terrible. The function of a ghost is to scare people, to inspire fear and dread in them. It is our pleasure and our responsibility. And students who questioned this most basic concept could be assured of a strict punishment: They were, in all likelihood, forced to spend an hour bottled up in a pickle jar like a genie. (*To this day I don't understand the reasoning behind this. But reason has little to do with most punishment, I suppose.*)

Anyone who had doubts about what a ghost's duties were could also be expelled from school. Without a

diploma, we were told, one could not find a well-paying job and would be forced to make do with the work offered to unskilled ghost laborers.

I tried hard to keep my mind on something other than the approaching midnight hour during my last two classes. I couldn't afford to voice my opinions like that again.

Only after we were on our way home from school did I again think about what was awaiting me that night. I let Lily and the Bag children float farther and farther ahead of me, and as we got closer to the castle, I moved more and more slowly. It wouldn't have taken much for me simply to float off into the woods.

When I finally arrived at the dungeon, Mama, Papa, Grandmama, Grandfather, and Lily had already sat down to lunch.

"We were beginning to think you weren't coming home at all," Papa rumbled, not knowing how close he was to the truth.

While the others enjoyed their meal, I only picked

at the food on my plate without having any idea what I was eating.

"Son," Papa began by clearing his throat the way he did when something important was about to be said. "You'll see that it's really not as difficult as you think." He laughed a little and put his hand on my shoulder. "To the contrary, it's quite simple once you get the hang of it."

"You're wasting your time," Grandfather grumbled.

Papa gave him a nasty look before he spoke again. "You've learned how to scare people in school, haven't you?"

I nodded and quickly recited: "It has to do, of course, with what kind of spirit you are. A werewolf has different methods at his disposal than a poltergeist. In my case I can roll my eyes around in my head, blow myself up to twice my normal size, howl horribly, gnash my teeth—"

"Is that enough to scare a person today?" Grandfather asked.

But Papa just ignored him
this time. "Good, good," he
said to me. "You only have to
apply what you've learned
and practiced in school."

"It's absolutely useless,"
Grandfather murmured.
"You'll make fools of your-
selves, that's all. If you don't succeed, everyone will
laugh at you. And you know what that could lead to—"

Grandmama interrupted him. "If you can't keep
quiet," she said angrily, "I'm going to put your head
outside under the bucket again!"

Insulted by this, Grandfather got up and headed off
to his room. I guessed he was going to take his midnight nap, but he left his head on the table.

What surprised me was that Grandmama appeared
to agree with Papa's plans for me. I looked at Mama,
who had promised to talk Papa out of the whole thing,
but she avoided my desperate look.

"In my opinion," Grandfather's head said, "there is

absolutely no reason to teach Max how to be a proper ghost. Sooner or later the time for ghosts will come to an end. It has probably happened already and just not caught up with us yet."

"Don't talk like that in front of the children," Mama growled. "Sometimes you are impossssible! Just think what would happen if the children repeated some of the things you say at home. Really, the way you carry on!"

As I sat there, my ears got bigger and bigger. Grandfather often talked like that in a roundabout way, but he had never been so direct before.

"Am I not right?" the head asked. "Times have changed; it's the end of an era."

"Be quiet now; now be quiet," Grandmama demanded.

"I wouldn't think of it," said Grandfather's head. "People don't believe in ghosts anymore, so it naturally follows that they're no longer afraid of us."

Papa grabbed me by the arm. "Come on, we're leaving!" And before I had a chance to wriggle free, he

pulled me through the dungeon and out the door.

Once on the steps, he loosened his grip enough for me to get away from him and glide back down into the dungeon.

"You said you would talk him out of it!" I howled at Mama.

She explained that all the ghosts in our area had heard about Papa and Uncle Dragul's bet. "Papa can't withdraw it now; you can understand that," she said. "Get ahold of yourself, Max. You mustn't make us look ridiculous. And another thing: Try not to exaggerate, you do let yourself get carried away. If you can frighten just one person even a little bit, I think that would satisfy everyone. If you can do that, you'll never need to try it again. . . ."

Grandfather's head opened its mouth, but before it could say anything, Grandmama turned the soup pot over it. All that could be heard was a soft babbling followed by a scornful laugh.

63

From the small hill where we touched down, we could see the entire village.

"Take a moment to study the layout of the streets," Papa said. "We're in no hurry."

It was a fairly small village. There was a church with a high, pointed steeple and a graveyard behind it; a ring of houses that encircled the church; an area where smaller houses with tiny gardens were nestled on tree-lined streets; and an outlying section in which there were a few scattered farmsteads with barns and stalls for animals. That was all.

I was relieved to see from our vantage point that it was a poorly lit village—nothing like the bright lights of the cities pictured in our schoolbooks. We observed

lights in only one house, the one situated next to the church. All the other houses were dark. There were streetlamps throughout the village, but the glow surrounding them wasn't at all as terrible as I had imagined.

"Why do people light their streets?" I asked, because it had never been explained to us at school.

"Because people can't see in the dark," Papa answered.

"But people are in their homes at night," I said. "Why do they need light where they aren't?"

"Well, because . . ." Papa began to say, but he didn't seem to have a good answer, so he growled, "Don't ask so many questions! It's time to practice what we'll soon put into action. Let's see, we'll begin by blowing ourselves up."

So I held my breath and began to expand. I grew bigger and bigger. When I was twice my normal size and thought I was going to burst, Papa signaled me to stop.

"Wonderful!" He praised me. "You look horrible and

frightening, very, very frightening. If you don't scare people looking this way, then I don't know what will. Now try howling."

I howled—first like a storm blowing through an old brick wall, then like a wolf. And then I rehearsed all twenty-seven of the easy and not-so-easy types of howls that we had learned in school. (You're not expected to know the twelve hard howls until you're graduated.)

Papa counted as I howled and was very pleased. "All twenty-seven, bravo! You didn't forget a single one. I'm proud of you, Son!"

I knew that he was praising me to give me courage. But it wasn't really necessary because at that moment— *I remember it so clearly*—I was determined to do what was expected of me. Mama had promised that if I succeeded that night, I would never have to spook again, so I knew what I had to do.

Papa also wanted me to practice gnashing my teeth, so I gnashed until he was happy. He even told me I was so convincing that *his* hair stood on end, just a little.

"The important thing," he explained, "is that you

get people's hair to bristle. If they're scared, it will stand on end. You know you're on the right track when chills run down their spines and the blood freezes in their veins. Whenever possible, scare a person senseless. All this can be done, Max, just by howling and gnashing your teeth. You'll see! We're ready now. Let's get to work!"

For a moment my fears came rushing back. But when I thought about the few hundred years of completely unghostlike life that had been promised me if I, just one time, performed my "ghostly duty," I was able to summon my courage.

Papa had eagerly flown off, so I followed. We glided down the hill, circled over the village once, and landed on one of the more dimly lit streets.

"Go ahead," Papa whispered, "start howling."

I knew if I let myself think too much about it, I'd be afraid again and wouldn't be able to make a sound.

"Go ahead," I repeated for encouragement, and I started to howl.

I tried about nineteen different howls. I would have

gotten an A plus in school, but there, in the village, on that small street, I was a total failure.

"Louder!" Papa demanded.

I howled louder. I howled louder than I had ever howled—even louder than I had for the Higher Academy for Ghosts entrance examination. But my howls just weren't loud enough. Then—finally—a light went on in the house we were standing in front of. A man's head appeared at the window. "Get away from here!" he yelled. "You stupid beasts! Scram! Get lost!"

After that we heard a woman call, "What's going on out there?"

"What's going on," the man at the window said, "is that either a couple of cats are giving a concert or a dog is howling at the moon." We saw him look up for a moment. "There's no moon out  tonight," he continued. "It's got to be cats—get away from here! Beat it! Let us get back to sleep!"

Then he shut the window, and the light went out.

"That's disgraceful!" Papa groaned. "He thought you were a cat."

"But that was a wolf howl!" I yelled furiously. "That part at the end was the best wolf howl I've ever done. A wild, ferocious wolf couldn't do any better than that. I'll try it again, and you'll see, that guy will be stunned."

But Papa shook his head. "It won't work. That fellow in there has probably never heard a wolf howl in his life, so he has no idea what one sounds like. He *has* heard a cat howl, and that's why he'll think that any shrill, bloodcurdling sound is a howling cat. He doesn't have any more imagination than that, I'm afraid."

"So he's not afraid of me?" I asked.

Papa shook his head again. "People without fantasy are almost never afraid. They're not capable of imagining the truly horrible and frightening things that exist in this world."

We stood there for a while, not knowing what to do. Only then did it occur to me that the man at the window hadn't looked at all as dreadful as the people in

our schoolbooks. Those people's faces were red and often had grimacing expressions. That man was certainly not as pleasantly pale as a ghost, but he almost—except for his much too short upper eyeteeth—looked like Uncle Dragul. And as I thought about it, there was really nothing frightening about him.

I hadn't been afraid of that human! I was so angry that he had mistaken me for a cat that I forgot to be afraid!

We floated farther down the street. "We have to get into one of these houses," Papa said. "Once people see us, we'll certainly not be mistaken for alley cats!"

I stopped in shock. No way, I thought. I would never ever set foot in a human's house! Seeing one from a distance hadn't been that bad, but face-to-face, inside one of their homes—never!

Papa must have seen my fear return. "All right," he said, "I'll go first. We'll choose a house where you can look through the window and see what I'm doing. But then we're going into the next one together."

I had to promise to go along with the plan; I guess

he was afraid I'd float away. Then we looked around until we found a suitable house at the end of a darkened street.

The front door was barred shut, but Papa quickly established that the keyhole was empty.

I was astonished. "People are funny. They lock their doors and leave the keyholes uncovered. Does that make sense?"

"People can't creep through keyholes," Papa explained.

"What *can* people do then?" I wanted to know. "They can't see in the dark, they can't creep through keyholes . . ."

"They busy themselves making automobiles and doing all sorts of other useless things," Papa said. "But that's enough talk; the night will be over soon! Look through that window, and pay attention so you'll know what to do at the next house."

With a halfhearted nod, I glided over to the window he had pointed to. I watched Papa make himself very long and thin; he looked like a giant white earthworm.

His head bent toward the keyhole, and in a split second the entire length of his body disappeared through it.

From my place at the window I saw Papa return to his natural shape once he was inside. He was standing in a kind of hall and began listening at a number of different doors. Then he turned to the stairs. But his shirt brushed against a flower vase that stood on a small table.

The vase crashed to the floor, and a moment later a woman's voice could be heard: "Don't tell me you're finally home, you old guzzler?"

I watched Papa stop, a shocked expression on his face. And I also saw what he wasn't able to until a moment later: A woman appeared at the top of the staircase.

There was no doubt in my mind that she was a human, but she *did* look a little bit ghostly. She was wearing a white nightgown and was strongly built, like Mrs. Bag. On her head she wore curlers, the way Mama does after she has washed her hair.

"Every day the same thing!" the woman yelled. And

it sounded just like Mama fussing at Papa when he got home late from the tavern.

My father was finally able to see the woman, and I was pretty sure he didn't like what he saw.

"Every day the same thing," she grumbled again. The next thing I knew she had stomped down the stairs and brushed past Papa, who was standing there still looking bewildered.

"I'm going to break your habit once and for all," she screamed. "Drinking away all our money! Just wait, I'll show you!"

I was shocked to see the woman yank a hanger from the closet and begin beating  my father with it. Naturally it swished right through him (it's not easy for a person to beat up a ghost), but she didn't seem to notice.

"Stand still!" she kept shrieking. "It won't do you any good to try to get away from me. I'll get you yet!"

Papa blew himself up, but in her anger the woman paid no attention. "Sure, sure," she cried. "Go ahead and puff yourself up, you old show-off; then I'll be able to get a better swing at you." She continued to thrash at Papa, angrier than before.

When his first trick didn't work, Papa chose to shrivel up his body. "So!" the woman jeered. "Now you've decided to show yourself for what you really are—a pitiful old wretch!"

I closed my eyes. I couldn't stand to watch my father being mistreated any longer. After what seemed like hours, there was silence in the house.

Then, finally, I heard the woman call, "Where are you, you weakling? I know you're hiding, you miserable creature! Act like a man, and show yourself."

Thank all good ghosts, I thought, Papa has gotten away.

There was another period of silence, followed again by the woman's voice. "Hiding won't help you! You'll have to come out eventually, and when you do . . ."

When I opened my eyes, the woman was climbing

the stairs, still swinging the clothes hanger menacingly. In a flash Papa was standing beside me. "You escaped!" I said in a voice choked with emotion.

"Call it what you will," Papa growled. "Even a woman in a frenzy can't seriously hurt a ghost like me. But it's not pleasant to have a clothes hanger whiz back and forth through your body, you can take it from me!"

Papa gnashed his teeth, not to scare anyone at that point, but purely out of anger. "I've had enough," he grumbled. "ENOUGH ENOUGH ENOUGH! How could I have come to this? It never would have happened in the old days."

"I won't tell anyone that she beat you up." I promised him.

"How's that? What?" Papa asked, embarrassed. "Oh, yes, right, I understand. Thank you, Son."

"Are all human women like that?"

"No, of course not. Most of them are . . . well, much different, in any case." Lost in thought, he pulled at the hem of his shirt. He appeared not really to be sure *what* female humans were like.

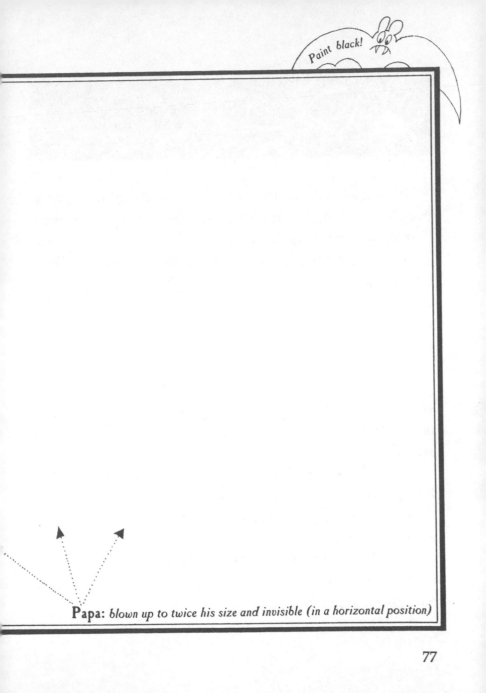

Paint black!

Papa: *blown up to twice his size and invisible (in a horizontal position)*

"Blast it all!" he swore. "I know it's difficult to frighten people these days, but I never would have imagined that it was like this."

I was astonished. "But you scare people every night," I said. "You must know what they're like."

"Not exactly every night," Papa said. "Some nights you don't even catch sight of one. Perhaps for several nights. . ."

"What do you do then?"

"Well, you know, I have to be there," Papa answered. "In the event that someone passes by and needs to be frightened, I'm ready. We call it being on standby."

If I had pressed further and asked more questions, I might have found out the whole truth then.

"If you ask me," I said, "the woman thought you were someone else."

"Her husband, I suppose," Papa said. "She was waiting for her husband. She heard something and naturally assumed it was he."

"But she must have noticed that you're not a human!"

"She was furious. When people are furious, their powers of observation are not good." Papa looked downcast, but his eyes suddenly lit up.

"I have an idea!" he whispered. "The man hasn't come home yet. The woman called him a guzzler. Where do you think you'd find a man who fits that description?"

"In the tavern . . ."

"Exactly, Son. That's where he must be," Papa beamed. "Come on."

He sailed down the street so fast that I had a hard time keeping up with him. Next to the church we stopped in front of a house, the only one in which I had seen lights burning earlier.

The sign hanging over the door said "Ye Olde Post Tavern." Realizing that it wasn't a house, I asked, "Is this the tavern Grandfather comes to?"

Papa nodded. "It belongs to the humans until shortly

after midnight, and after that we take our turn." We waited.

"The fellow has to come along soon," Papa said. "And we've got a head start because he's already afraid."

"Why?" I asked. "Of what?"

"His wife, of course. I'm sure he knows she's waiting for him at home, though he probably doesn't know about the hanger. Frightening someone who is already afraid shouldn't be too hard, even for you." Papa had his hand on my shoulder again. "Now show me that you're worthy of your ancestors, who were the most terrifying poltergeists the night has ever seen."

Again I remembered Mama's promise: that I'd never have to face another person again if I performed my duties acceptably.

The tavern door opened. Someone staggered out, almost stumbling on the edge of the pavement. The door was locked behind him. The man, whose wife was waiting for him at home with a clothes hanger, had been the last customer.

"Don't disappoint me!" I heard Papa whisper. Then

I found myself standing across from the man, all alone.

He didn't notice me at first. He was staring straight ahead, humming a song to himself and trying hard to stay on his feet.

"Boooo!" I cried, but the man only said, "What?"

He rubbed his half-closed eyes and said, "What?" once more. "What are you doing out on the street this late, my boy?" he added, after his eyes had opened and focused a little. "Don't you know that children are supposed to be in bed at this hour?"

"Boo-ooo-ooo!" I yelled as horribly as I possibly could.

But he only mumbled, "Now don't start crying!" (I was furious that he had mistaken my wail for crying.) "I won't hurt you," he said to me. "It's not for me to judge people who let their children run around the streets in the middle of the night. I don't concern myself with other people's business—"

"I'm not a child. I'm a ghost!" I screamed furiously. I proceeded to give my most impressive wolf howl.

The tipsy man only laughed. "Very good!" he praised me. "You do that very well. If a person were timid, he

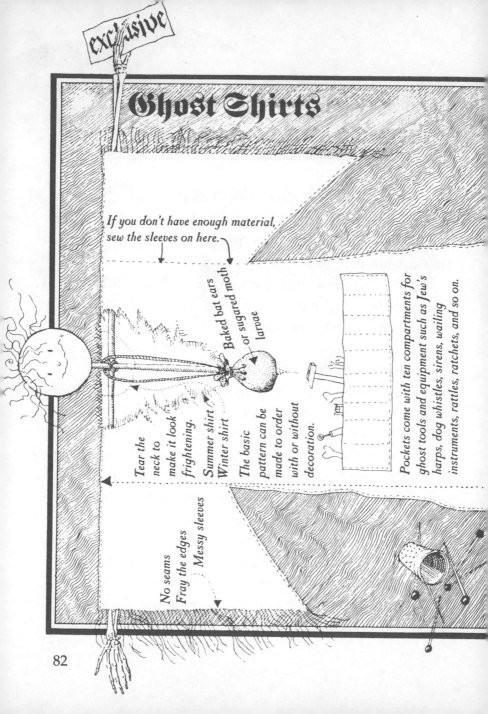

exclusive

If you don't have enough material, sew the sleeves on here.

Tear the neck to make it look frightening.

Summer shirt
Winter shirt

The basic pattern can be made to order with or without decoration.

Baked bat ears or sugared moth larvae

No seams
Fray the edges
Messy sleeves

Pockets come with ten compartments for ghost tools and equipment such as Jew's harps, dog whistles, sirens, wailing instruments, rattles, ratchets, and so on.

Materials:

Use white, thin material for best results (curtain material or cotton fabric, for example). A shirt of old sheets is heavier but so-o-o strong that it will last for many generations!

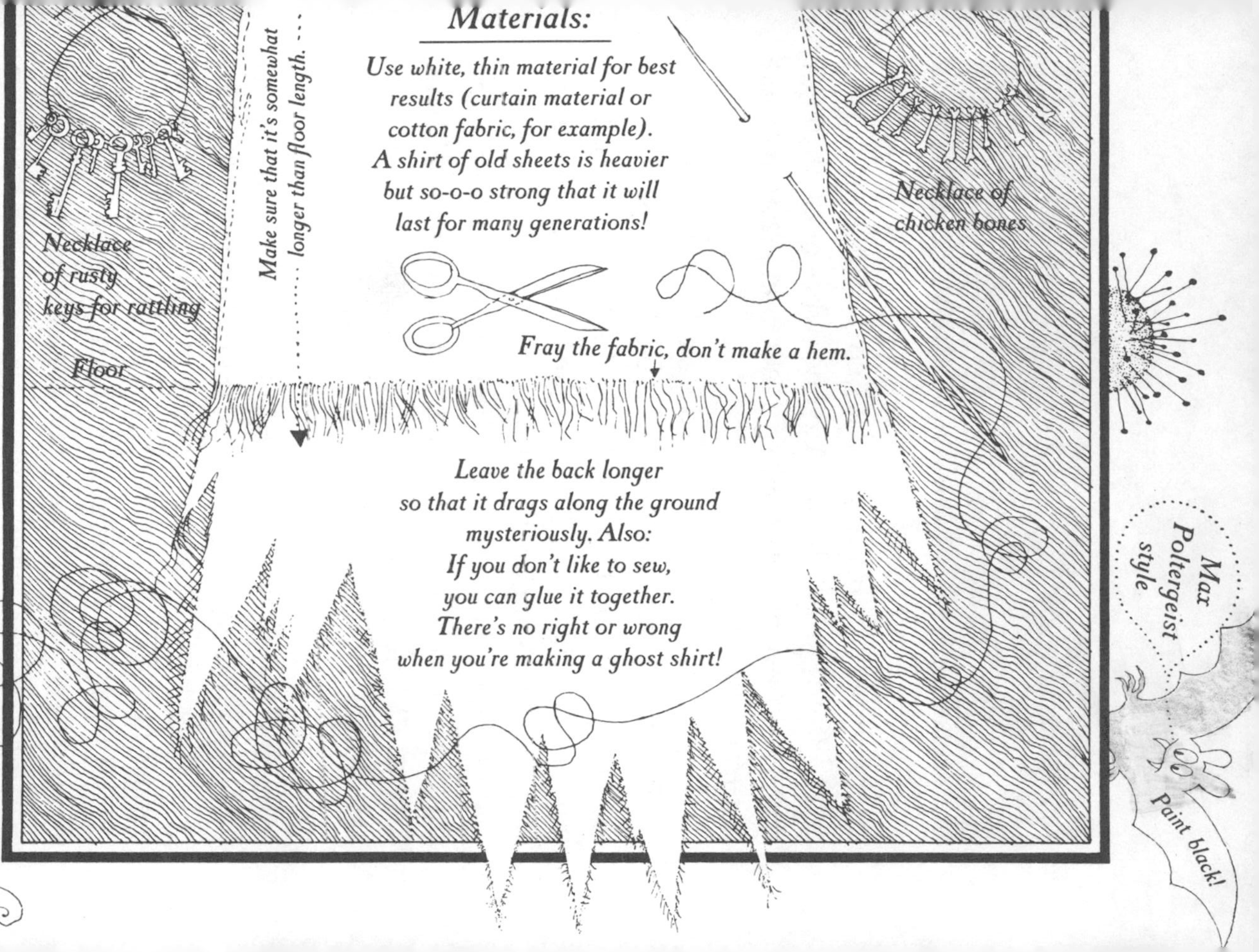

Necklace of rusty keys for rattling
Floor
Make sure that it's somewhat longer than floor length.
Necklace of chicken bones
Fray the fabric, don't make a hem.
Max Poltergeist style
Paint black!

Leave the back longer so that it drags along the ground mysteriously. Also: If you don't like to sew, you can glue it together. There's no right or wrong when you're making a ghost shirt!

might think you really were a ghost. But—hee-hee—I can't afford to be timid. Anyone who goes through what I do every night when I get home has learned not to be afraid.''

''I *am* a real ghost!'' I yelled again.

''But of course!'' the man mumbled. He staggered so far to one side that I thought he'd fall over. ''If a little boy puts a sheet over his head and yells 'booo,' then, of course, he's a ghost.''

With knees bent he addressed me at eye level. The smell of alcohol was so strong that I had to float back a step. ''I must admit, you could nearly pass for the real thing,'' he said with a grin. ''I did the same thing when I was your age—I'd put a white sheet over my head and run around scaring people. I know it's great fun, but now, my boy, I have to go. I'm late. My wife is waiting for me at home, and I'm sure she's worked herself into a rage.''

He turned around and was about to leave me there, alone on the street, when my father appeared by my side and yelled, ''Stop!''

The man did stop, but he didn't seem to know whether or not he should turn around. When he *did* turn back, what he saw caused him to freeze in shock. He then rubbed his eyes using his fists, and only after steadying himself did he let them again drop to his sides.

I did it! I thought with pride.

But then the man stammered, "Now there are two where before there was one. Oh, no, oh, no, I'm seeing double. It's just as my wife predicted. 'If you don't stop drinking,' she's always saying to me, 'you'll soon see where it will lead: First you'll see double, then you'll see white mice, and then—' No! Never again! I solemnly swear; I'll never drink again. Not a drop!"

The shock seemed to have sobered him. Although he could barely stand up minutes before, he suddenly straightened up and took off at a run. By the time Papa and I understood what had happened, he had already disappeared.

Once we got back to the dungeon, things went from bad to worse.

Grandfather delighted in telling us that he had foreseen the failure of Papa's scheme. And Grandmama continued to ramble about the family's reputation.

However, none of us knew at the time that Papa and I had been observed.

"You embarrassed yourselves in front of people; you embarrassed yourselves," Grandmama said. Because she felt the results of our unsuccessful attempts could be disastrous for the entire family, Grandmama decided to take matters into her own hands. "A situation like this calls for an old, experienced ghost; that's what it calls for. My grandson Max will have the benefit of

learning from my centuries of experience. We'll begin tomorrow right after school."

And so, on the next night, I found myself sitting with Grandmama on a bridge over the humans' superhighway.

"They'll be here soon," Grandmama said, and her eyes began to glow the way they did when she was particularly happy about something.

But she refused to tell me who was coming soon.

As the wind puffed out our shirts, cars zoomed by in opposite directions below us. The concrete strips of road seemed to go on forever. And on them the cars' lights cut harshly through the otherwise peaceful darkness, shining two beams of light far into the distance. I shut my eyes when the first few cars' lights neared the bridge, but I got used to their noise and lights soon enough.

"Do people travel all night long?" I asked, and Grandmama nodded.

"Where are all those cars going?" I continued, but Grandmama didn't have an answer for me.

"I really don't know," she said. "Cars have existed for only sixty or seventy years, cars have. I haven't had time to find out where they're going yet."

Grandmama held her nose after several cars had driven by one after another (there is no worse smell to a ghost than that of gas and exhaust fumes).

"I preferred the days when people traveled on foot or by horse," she sighed. "Those were the good old days. A hundred years ago traveling journeymen with no money had to sleep outdoors at night. Some of them even worked up the courage to sleep in the haunted ruins of castles. We would come upon them there and give them such a good scare. What fun it was. I liked the horsemen best; I liked them best. Horses almost always spook when they see a ghost. And when horses get spooked, their riders fall off. If you're lucky, they might even break their necks. I can't bear to think back on those wonderful times; I can't bear to think of it."

Grandmama was overcome by her memories and was deep in thought with her eyes closed. When a car passed under the bridge, the noise scared her so badly

that she almost fell from the railing onto the highway.

"Today," she complained in a somewhat shaken voice, "people shut themselves into those smelly tin crates. They're safe from us in there because not even the sneakiest, shiftiest ghost has figured out a way to get into one of them."

"When was the last time you scared a person?"

"Oh," Grandmama said, "it must have been during the time when people traveled by stagecoach. I didn't want to switch over to trains and cars at my age, so I retired. And I already had the five hundred years one needs for retirement, already had them."

Her answer took me by surprise. Grandmama always acted as though she rattled and howled at people every night.

"So what?" she said. Her question made me uncomfortable because it meant she was reading my mind again. "I show off a little. Every ghost does that."

I wondered if she meant that none of the others had scared anyone in a long time either. . . .

"That's exactly what I mean." Grandmama answered

my thoughts again. "Take your father, for example. A poltergeist, a very talented poltergeist he is. But what could he expect to do to a person these days? People haven't been afraid of spooks and unexplained noises for a long time. Now if they hear something in their house, they think the heating system isn't working. Their only fear is that their cars might break down."

Why is she telling me this? I thought. Why tonight?

"Because you're old enough now," Grandmama answered. "And because tonight is the night that you must prove yourself; prove yourself you must."

"Prove myself! Why? Why should I learn something that others don't practice anymore?"

"Because no matter what, you have to accept your responsibilities as a ghost!" Grandmama was suddenly strict.

I recalled my conversation with Mama the night before, but Grandmama wouldn't let me finish the thought. "Your mother is absolutely correct. If you hadn't admitted your fear of people, you could have saved your-

self this trouble. Take your sister, Lily. Because she's always chattering about how much she likes to frighten people with her screams, no one expects her to prove it; no one expects it. As a matter of fact, everyone is happy that she doesn't try to. These days there is danger in every such attempt."

She was suddenly quiet, as though she were sorry she'd said so much.

"What danger?" I asked a few times. Now that Grandmama had begun, I wanted to know everything, everything!

"Maybe you're right," she said.

"So, what danger is there?"

"The danger of failure, of course. It could turn out that we are no longer able to scare people. And that would mean we've become totally useless, is what that would mean."

I understood. Every further attempt to scare someone could bring new proof that we—

"Right!" Grandmama interrupted my thoughts again. "And thanks to your father's silly bet, you now have

to prove that people have not yet outgrown the spirit world."

That was too much for me, too much at one time. Suddenly I understood so much and, at the same time, felt I knew so little. . . .

"You can depend on me!" Grandmama said comfortingly. "I have a few hundred years of experience, I have."

"But not with the people of today!"

"I have studied some of the ways of people today," Grandmama said defensively.

After a while I asked her again whom she had summoned. She seemed to think it was time to tell me, but just at that moment she cried out, "There they are, finally!"

She pointed straight ahead, to where the concrete lanes of the highway split a forest in two. Far ahead I could see a blue, flashing light that disappeared, then reappeared as it rapidly approached us.

Grandmama giggled with pleasure. Jumping into the air, she called, "Come on, Max!" and fluttered away.

I followed her over the highway, wondering what other choice I had.

"It's the police. I summoned them," she whispered excitedly. "Right now they're safely tucked inside their car, but I've thought of something to lure them out. . . ."

The police! I thought. According to what I had heard in school up to that point, this type of human was big and strong and had experienced all sorts of frightening things. Surely it would not be easy to scare someone like that.

"You're wrong there, my dear Max!" Grandmama corrected me. "Very often those people who feel strong and important because of the jobs they do are the ones most easily scared."

"I hope you're right," I said.

We flew a short distance until we came to a small road that shot off from the superhighway. After winding around in a big circle, it flowed into a street on which people didn't drive as fast. We landed where the two streets met. We were to wait there for the police to arrive, Grandmama told me. And when they did,

they'd be in for a night that they wouldn't forget for the rest of their lives.

"I called them on the telephone and said that a terrible accident had occurred on this corner," Grandmama said proudly, and her eyes glowed again. "We'll lie down at the edge of the road, we'll lie down. The police will come, and they'll see two ghostly pale figures lying here. They'll have to get out of their tin crate whether they like it or not. It's their duty, it is. And then . . . boo-ooo!"

"All right," I said, and lay down near her in the dewy grass on the side of the road. Somehow I didn't feel right about what we were doing. The night before, my fear of people had given me a stomachache. That night it was the hopeless feeling that the entire future of the spirit community might depend on what was about to happen. And on top of everything, I still didn't like the idea of scaring people.

We lay there for a few minutes in silence. Then Grandmama raised her head and said, "Surely those idiots didn't take the wrong exit!"

A few more minutes went by before we finally saw the blue light.

"You know what to do!" Grandmama whispered.

"Of course," I said. "I'm to do what a ghost must do."

"This will be great fun; it will be!" she said happily.

"We'll wait until they bend over us, and then—"

The police car stopped. I peeked with one eye and saw two men get out. Their faces didn't look much different from the men's I had seen the night before. But they weren't dressed like the others. Both wore dark clothes with lots of shiny buttons and had particularly funny caps on their heads.

One man was as round as a balloon; the other one, very thin.

"There's something lying up ahead," I heard the thin one say.

"Do you have your flashlight?" the stout one asked.

The thin one didn't answer, but in his hand a light clicked on. It was so terribly bright that I had to squeeze my eyes shut.

I heard their steps coming nearer and nearer. I held

my breath and started counting backward from one hundred.

Grandmama whispered, "Now!"

Without hesitating, I rose right in front of the thin policeman and screamed, "Boo! Boo! Boo!" with everything I could put into it.

At the same time Grandmama let out so wretched a howl that it sent chills down *my* spine.

But the two policemen weren't spooked. The stout one took a step back and shouted, "Quiet!" scaring me so much that my fourth "Boo!" got stuck in my throat.

"What is the meaning of this?" screamed the thin policeman.

"You'll soon see; see you will!" Grandmama shrieked, and looked as though she were about to throw herself on the one who resembled a balloon, perhaps to frighten him with her ice-cold breath.

However, the two policemen threw themselves on Grandmama first. Before I knew what was happening, the stout one had grabbed the right sleeve of her smock, the thin one her left.

I thought it would be easy for Grandmama to escape their grip. She had only to make herself small and thin to wriggle free. But for some reason, she wasn't able to. Her face twisted with the effort, but her form hardly changed at all.

She's too old, I thought. That's the only explanation. Old ghosts can't alter their forms as easily as young ghosts can.

Grandmama howled again—this time in anger, but rather than bloodcurdling, it sounded pitiful.

"Be quiet, my good woman!" the thin policeman said. Strangely enough, he sounded quite friendly. But Grandmama got so angry about being called "my good woman" that she continued to howl until the stout policeman tried to put his hand over her mouth.

Looking back on the scene, I know that I should have found some way to help Grandmama. But of course,

it's always easier to know what to do after it's too late to do it.

I was so startled that it never occurred to me to do something.

But what happened next was more surprising still.

Almost at the same time both policemen were hit by a blast of the ice-cold air that Grandmama's body naturally gives off. That will do the trick, I thought. Instead, the stout one said something about the woman being unusually cold, and the thin one said that he wasn't surprised. "The poor thing must have gotten a chill lying in the wet grass."

"Something's not right here," the big man said. I was beginning to get hopeful until he added, "What are an old woman and a boy doing on the road at this hour, wearing nothing but nightshirts?"

I waited for Grandmama to do something. But she remained quietly where she was. Her failure had totally confused her.

"We'll get the personal data first," the thin policeman

said. "That's always a good thing to do when you don't know what else to do."

Grandmama didn't move when he let her go to pull out his notepad. But her eyes were glowing again, so I was fairly sure she had come up with a new plan.

"What is your name, my good woman?" the thin man asked.

And Grandmama answered softly, "Poltergeist. Yolanda Theodora Genevieve Poltergeist."

The thin policeman let a laugh escape from his pinched lips; then he cleared his throat. "Forgive me," he said, "I know it's impolite to laugh at someone's name. After all, you didn't pick it out for yourself."

He had Grandmama repeat her name as he wrote it down on his notepad. After that he wanted to know her birthdate.

"Of course, one shouldn't ask such a question of a lady," he added. "Let me assure you that my interest is purely within the line of duty."

Grandmama smiled at him and answered, "I was born on February 29, 1211."

"Surely you mean 1911," the thin policeman said.

"I mean 1211," Grandmama responded.

"But that would make you . . . more than seven hundred years old."

"So I am."

The stout policeman let go of Grandmama's smock. Taking a step back, he tapped his forehead with his index finger. It seemed to be a sign to the other policemen that Grandmama was not meant to see.

I didn't know what that meant, but the thin policeman appeared to understand. A smile spread across his face. Then he snapped his notepad shut, asked us to wait for a moment, and went to the car. Talking into a telephone-like piece of equipment, he said, "We've picked up two strange ones, an old lady and a kid, both in nightshirts. The old lady, by the way, maintains she's over seven hundred years old."

He listened to the high-pitched voice that came out

of the speaker box, then laughed. "That's just what I thought myself. They're two loonies, probably escaped from the hospital—"

"We are *not* crazy!" Grandmama shrieked. "We are ghosts, clever and terrifying ghosts at that, clever and terrifying."

Grandmama's outburst seemed to amuse the stout policeman. "That's what you look like in those nightshirts," he laughed.

The thin one spoke into the phone. "We were just told by the old lady that they're ghosts. . . . Yes, yes, I know, crazies always have wild imaginations. . . . All right, we'll hold them until the funny wagon gets here. And tell them to bring a couple of blankets—the old lady is ice-cold, frozen solid."

Our only hope was for Grandmama to make herself invisible.

Scarcely had the thought crossed my mind when she disappeared. She didn't actually vanish; she just couldn't be seen. I knew she was still there because the stout policeman's gold-braided cap suddenly lifted off his

head and sailed in a wide arc across the street. Right after that his right ear began to stretch (it looked so rubbery, I thought it might get as long as a rabbit's). Grandmama must have been angrily pulling on it because his cries of pain were loud and shrill.

The thin one attempted to come to his aid, but he tripped over something that he didn't see—which happened to be Grandmama's leg—and fell on his face.

When the stout policeman tried to help the thin one to his feet, he lost his balance and fell forward (Grandmama must have kicked him in the backside), landing beside the thin one on the street.

The next thing I knew Grandmama and I were in the dungeon. Thank all good ghosts, she had remembered one of her ancient tricks that not only got us out of our tight spot but also saved us from the long trip home.

"You can't let yourself be bullied, you can't," Grandmama explained to the family. She had repeated the story about our encounter with the police three times, and each time it got more fantastic.

Grandmama was on her fourth telling. She was describing how she had lifted the policemen sixty feet into the air and let them drop. But when she said that the fat policeman had bounced like a rubber ball and rolled away, Mama interrupted her.

"We all know how wonderful you were," she said impatiently. "But now it's time to help me clean up. All of you can lend a hand."

Right before Grandmama and I returned to the dungeon, an owl had brought a message saying that Aunt

Lilofee planned to drop in for a visit. She was at the dentist with little Alfred and wanted to stop by for fifteen minutes on their way home.

"She'll be here any minute," Mama said urgently, "and it looks i-m-p-o-s-s-s-s-i-b-l-e in here, like a pigsty."

Papa had just come home from work. He seemed quite pleased by what Grandmama told him. Rather than be bothered that it was Grandmama, not I, who had confronted the police, he felt my being there was more important than anything else. No one needed to know exactly what had happened, he said.

"He's going to look ridiculous, old Dragul, when he hears he has lost the bet. I'd give anything to see the expression on his face." Papa grinned. "Don't tell Lilofee what happened right away," he said to Grandmama and me. "We'll bring it up casually, as though it were nothing special—"

"You should all be helping me clean up!" Mama said again, her voice dangerously sharp.

Papa looked around in astonishment. "Mama's right. It's a mess in here. How does it happen? When a wife

is at home all night, the apartment should always be neat and clean . . ."

He shouldn't have gone that far. Mama bared her long eyeteeth, and it looked as if she were going to give Papa a deadly bite. I suppose the only reason she didn't try was that she knew that a vampire bite couldn't do damage to a ghost. Instead, she let loose a scream that matched Lily's best.

"All right, all right," Papa said. "I only meant . . . what I wanted to say was . . . that on one hand, you're always talking about getting a part-time job, but on the other hand, you can't even take care of the house—" Papa didn't get any farther than that because he had to duck to avoid being hit by a pair of boots that had been thrown in his direction. As it was, they missed his head only by inches.

"Who left his IMPOSSSSIBLY muddy boots in the middle of the dungeon?" Mama shrieked. Then it was Lily, busy with her poisonous spiders, who was forced to watch for flying objects. A couple of notebooks whizzed past her ears as Mama screamed, "And who

left these schoolbooks lying around?" I quickly re-
moved my books from the table.

But Mama wasn't about to stop there. "Grandfather
simply leaves his head wherever it drops." I was just
barely able to keep her from throwing Grandfather's
own head at him.

"What a she-devil!" Papa cried with delight. "What
a temper!" His whole face lit up. "What I love about
you most, my dear, is that you can't control that furious
temper of yours."

But Mama wasn't furious. In fact, she looked as though
she were about to cry. "I do nothing all night long
besides horrible, boring housework," she said softly to
herself. "Then this IMPOSSSSIBLE fool comes home
and . . ." Then she did begin to cry."He hangs around
all night on so-called standby, knocks around a little
here, a little there, gets annoyed because there's nobody who'll listen to him, then comes home and
says—"

Papa tried to change the subject. "I didn't mean it
that way."

Mama turned to Grandmama and said, "Do I have to put up with this?"

But Grandmama didn't respond. Rather, she began rattling on about the police again.

So Mama began to whirl around the apartment like a tornado. Usually she carried on like that only outside, but this time she kept going until I was afraid the dungeon walls would fall down around us.

"Enough, enough already," Papa said. "We'll help you clean up." The storm that was my mother slowed to a stop and we all went to work. Grandmama straightened up. Lily hung new spider webs because the old ones looked a little ragged. I watered the walls until they were nicely slimy and the white mold shone. In less than ten minutes the dungeon looked the way an apartment  belonging to a family of orderly spooks should.

Just as we finished, there was a rumbling sound

outside, followed by a cry of pain. Shortly after that Aunt Lilofee and little Alfred—who was rubbing his shins—appeared in the dungeon. As always, he was neatly dressed, but his tails were completely covered with yellowish green slime.

"He slipped on the steps," Aunt Lilofee said, a little embarrassed. "He's not used to such narrow stairs. As you know, the staircases in our castle are FAAABU-LOUSLY, comfortably wide. And by the way, your steps outside are awfully slippery."

"Yes," Mama laughed. "I have to soak them with bucketfuls of water every night, or they wouldn't smell so dank and moldy."

"But you could break your neck," little Alfred griped.

"Not us," said Lily. "We don't have to climb stairs on foot the way vampires do. We just float over them."

Mama invited them to sit down, while Aunt Lilofee began to tell us how pleased the dentist had been with little Alfred. "His upper eyeteeth have grown FAAA-BULOUSLY. We'll be able to begin filing them soon. We needn't worry anymore, the dentist said. He is

certain that one night our Alfred will be a perfectly FAAABULOUS vampire."

"Yes, well, we're also very proud of our Max," Papa said, and I could clearly see that he wanted to bring up the bet. But for the moment he said nothing more.

We had been chatting for a few minutes when Aunt Lilofee asked if we knew why so many policemen were out that night.

For Papa the time to talk about his victory had come, but Grandmama spoke up before he had a chance. "*I* can tell you about that, my dear Lilofee!" she cried. "The police are out because there's been quite a lot going on tonight. Max and I had them running around in circles. We did such a fine job frightening them that they're probably still in shock."

"I didn't get that impression at all," Aunt Lilofee said, affecting an English accent. "It was my understanding that they were looking for someone. To be more precise, I heard they were searching for two mental ward escapees . . . wearing nightshirts."

"Nonsense!" Grandmama hissed. "They're just say-

ing that because they don't want to admit how afraid they were; they're afraid to admit—"

"An old woman and a child were mentioned," Aunt Lilofee continued. Then she stopped short, and her voice turned syrupy, "Surely they're not talking about you?" She pointed to Grandmama and me. "Oh, my goodness, how embarrassing to be mistaken as crazy people by humans."

Grandfather had been listening silently to all this, but suddenly he let out a laugh that filled the room. "That's the way it is today. In the old days people thought spirits, ghosts, and witches were behind everything, even behind things that had natural explanations. Today just the opposite is true. People think there has to be a natural explanation for everything, even when a ghost is responsible and happy to take the credit."

"I just hope that word doesn't get around any more than it has already," Aunt Lilofee said. "There are those who say you made laughingstocks of us all last night."

"Who says that?" Papa wanted to know.

"Well," Aunt Lilofee hedged. "There's a rumor in

the air . . . but it's probably best not to pay attention to that sort of thing."

"That's right," Mama cried. "So many ghosts are just imposssssible! They don't seem to have anything better to do than slander others."

"That's what I always say," Aunt Lilofee agreed. "And besides, I don't believe what they're saying—"

"What are you talking about?" Papa asked uneasily.

"We heard that you, my dear brother-in-law, were beaten up by a woman last night. But as I said, I don't believe a word of it. A grown ghost like you would certainly never allow himself to be beaten by a human, especially one that was female. It would be ridiculous to think something like that had actually happened. We all know that once a ghost humiliates himself, he's washed up as a spook."

"The woman didn't know that I was a ghost. She mistook me for her husband," Papa cried, then stopped short because he became aware of the silence that had settled into the dungeon. Everyone was looking at him.

A minute went by, then another and another. Papa

stared down at the tablecloth. He finally raised his head and laughed as if to say, things aren't as bad as they seem. But his laugh sounded embarrassed.

Like a furious storm breaking loose, Mama, Grandmama, Aunt Lilofee, and even Lily started screaming at Papa. They said that he was a disgrace to ghosts, that the damage he had done was perhaps beyond repair.

At the same time, a few other ghouls were coming to similar conclusions. Some of the most influential spirits in the area had gathered in the village cemetery, but it was not until much later that we received a

detailed account of their meeting. The werewolf who lived in a forest far away from all human settlements was there. Half human, half wolf, he had a hairy face, the long, fanged teeth of a wild animal, and sharp claws instead of fingernails.

A skeleton, wrapped in a ragged black coat, was

sitting on a tombstone. Whenever it got excited, its old yellow bones would rattle and clink.

A huge black dog with glowing red eyes ran up and down among the graves, up and down like a lion in a cage. Now and then it growled, foam dripping from its mouth.

Two hobgoblins, tiny men with weathered, shriveled-up faces, jumped excitedly from grave marker to grave marker.

Shadows darted over the earth and the gravestones, withering flowers left on the graves as they passed. The shadows didn't belong to bodies; they were simply spirits.

Even the man from the deep was there. He appeared on land only every two hundred years or so because his green, shiny body—which jiggled and glittered, constantly changing shape—couldn't survive out of water for long.

Under a cypress tree an open casket had been laid on the cemetery wall. In it was a pale, still man with a knife stuck deep in his chest.

116

He was the most powerful of the ghouls assembled there, all of whom I had heard about but never seen. The stories told about them were so frightening they'd shaken the confidence of braver ghosts than I.

In my wildest dreams I never would have imagined that these ghouls would be gathered so close to our castle, discussing, of all things, my father and me.

In the meantime, the screeching had died down in our dungeon.

"How dare you talk to me like that—and in front of the children?" Papa yelled at them, ignoring the fact that Lily—who *was* one of the children—was hollering at him as well. They remained silent, but all eyes were focused on Papa.

Mama broke the spell by suggesting that we children go play outside. Her tone of voice left no room for debate. So out we crept.

"They always send us away just when it gets inter-

esting!" Lily grumbled as we sat in the courtyard.

I hovered nearby, afraid without being able to understand my feelings. What I had gone through the last two nights had been simply too much for me. All of a sudden my whole world was falling apart.

Three nights before, I believed that my parents and grandparents were extraordinarily successful spooks. Now I knew that not one of them had taught a human being the meaning of fear for a long time. Why, then, did they insist I learn something that they had stopped practicing long ago?

Why were they teaching us things in school that we would never need to know? At the beginning of my ordeal I had still been afraid of people. But by that night I had faced up to them on two occasions and had learned they weren't any more frightening than ghosts. Why, then, I wondered, were they made to look so frightening in our schoolbooks? And why should we scare people when, after all, they didn't do us any harm?

"People need to be frightened every now and then;

otherwise they become arrogant," said Lily, who had learned a little about reading minds from Grandmama.

"Nonsense!" little Alfred said. "People aren't scared by us anymore. They're not even afraid of my dad."

Later, when we were given the full details of that evening, we realized that at the same time the adults were carrying on a heated discussion in our dungeon, the meeting at the cemetery was equally as serious.

They all had agreed—the werewolf, the skeleton, the black dog, the hobgoblins, the shadows, and the man from the deep—that my father had jeopardized the future of the spirit world.

"Just imagine," the werewolf growled, "what would have happened if the woman had noticed she was beating up a ghost rather than her husband."

"She might have laughed at him," the smaller of the hobgoblins added with a screech.

"If a human laughs at a spirit even once, we're all finished!" the skeleton continued, tiny flames dancing furiously in his empty eye sockets.

"We're all very much aware of that," the man from

← This is the way to mak
lovely shadows. To make ther
even **more** "bodiless," hang the black paper figure
on a string, and let them dance in front of a lamp
(Don't forget to make legs.

120

This picture isn't scary because it's printed in red! After you find out which things are supposed to be black, take a felt-tip pen, and color over them. It's your job to make this picture dark and creepy!!!

the deep said impatiently. "We must decide what is to be done. I'm beginning to dry up."

"Yes, what is to be done?" a few shadows echoed.

"This poltergeist must be punished!" the black dog barked, rolling its fiery eyes. "He should have known better than to make a drunken bet on a thing as serious as frightening humans."

"On the other hand, one can understand why he wants to teach his son about the meaning of our existence," a deep black shadow suggested.

"We have to make sure that poltergeists and other harmless ghosts stay that way in the future," the were-wolf yapped. "Only those spirits selected as the most loathsome, the most dreadful, and the most wolflike should be allowed to approach people."

"I see you've included yourself," a hobgoblin giggled.

"Of course," the werewolf howled.

Then the hobgoblin reminded him that even he, at one time, had been in danger of being laughed at by a human.

"I don't deny that the situation with humans has become difficult," the werewolf said, "but for that very reason, simple poltergeists should no longer be allowed to scare people—"

He was interrupted by the black dog. "This idiot poltergeist has to be punished!" it again demanded. "He puts us all in danger, and if we don't teach him a lesson now, he may yet succeed in causing our downfall. If we're forced to give up frightening people, life as we know it will come to an end."

The black dog's words settled the matter for the werewolf, the skeleton, the hobgoblins, the shadows, and the man from the deep. That's when they began to think about suitable punishments.

Then the man from the deep, who wanted to get the whole thing over with quickly because he was becoming drier and drier by the minute, said, "We should simply eliminate this poltergeist and his whole family from the picture. We have to make sure they're never able to put us in this position again. I suggest we wall them up in their dungeon."

Vampire Shirt

(for ghost parties)

Mathilda's Design

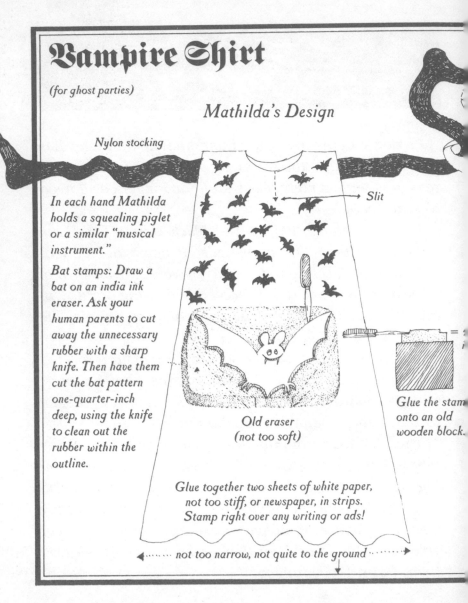

Nylon stocking

→ Slit

In each hand Mathilda holds a squealing piglet or a similar "musical instrument."

Bat stamps: Draw a bat on an india ink eraser. Ask your human parents to cut away the unnecessary rubber with a sharp knife. Then have them cut the bat pattern one-quarter-inch deep, using the knife to clean out the rubber within the outline.

Old eraser
(not too soft)

Glue the stamp onto an old wooden block.

Glue together two sheets of white paper, not too stiff, or newspaper, in strips. Stamp right over any writing or ads!

◄ ········ not too narrow, not quite to the ground ········ ►

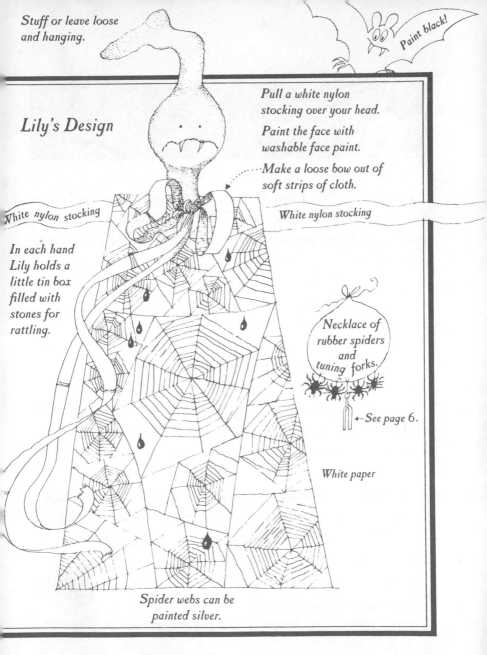

Stuff or leave loose and hanging.

Paint black!

Lily's Design

Pull a white nylon stocking over your head.

Paint the face with washable face paint.

Make a loose bow out of soft strips of cloth.

White nylon stocking

White nylon stocking

In each hand Lily holds a little tin box filled with stones for rattling.

Necklace of rubber spiders and tuning forks.

←See page 6.

White paper

Spider webs can be painted silver.

At about that time it was pretty quiet back at the dungeon. Alfred, Lily, and I had crept down the steps and were listening at the old iron gate. No one was screaming.

We entered the dungeon as Papa was saying, "Maybe you're right. Maybe we should accept Uncle Percy's invitation and go to England."

"For a short time anyway," Mama added. "Perhaps for only two or three hundred years, until the story's forgotten."

Grandfather grinned. I got the feeling he was thinking about the brands of Scotch whisky he'd developed such a taste for.

Aunt Lilofee spoke up. "We've also been thinking about leaving. My dear Dragul is such a restless spirit; he hates to stay anywhere for more than a hundred years. We thought perhaps we would spend some time in Dragul's homeland, Transylvania. That's if we don't accept the FAAABULOUS offer to go to America that Dragul got not long ago."

She didn't say what kind of offer it was. But the

others weren't interested anyway; they had enough troubles of their own to worry about.

"In two or three hundred years," Mama said to Papa, "no one will remember that you were beaten up by a woman. Then we can return if we want to."

"Sooner or later we would have had to look for a new apartment, sooner or later," Grandmama said. "In a few months the people will be finished with their construction. Then they'll make our castle into a hotel, and our dungeon will be turned into the wine cellar. There'll be no room left for us at all."

As their conversation dragged on, I realized our move to England was as good as decided.

And not so far away, it was as good as decided that we were to be walled up in our dungeon. Every ghoul had agreed with the man from the deep. Only the man in the coffin remained to be heard.

He listened while the others talked about the numerous and hideous ways in which we could be punished in addition to being walled in. Then, finally, the man in the coffin decided to speak.

He actually succeeded in moving his right hand, which was a feat because it was said that he could move nothing more than his mouth. To silence the others, he knocked three times on the side of his coffin. Then he spoke in a slow and heavy voice. "The poltergeist, whom you wish to bury alive with his family, has done nothing dishonorable."

We were told that his voice sounded far away, as though it were rising from a bottomless grave. "He tried to do what he has done for centuries. Are we to punish him for attempting to carry out what is, in fact, his duty? Is he wrong in wishing to teach his son responsibility?"

Despite their great respect for the man in the coffin, the other spirits hotly disagreed.

But the man in the coffin wouldn't budge. "What happened to that poltergeist could happen to any other ghost tomorrow . . . and has already to many. We simply have not faced the facts until now." In the account we later received, we were told that the man in the coffin's stiff upper body lent a certain dignity to his words.

"No longer can we act as though things today are as they were a hundred years ago," he continued. "We must adjust ourselves to this new world. Perhaps there are a handful of particularly dreadful spirits that can still frighten certain timid humans. But we cannot allow ourselves to be deceived. If the smallest, most harmless ghost is not able to achieve spook status, then we must accept reality. The time for ghosts may soon be over."

"What do you suggest?" asked the skeleton, his bones rattling.

"The smallest, most harmless ghost within our community is Max Poltergeist. He must find a human to frighten. He must accept the challenge, and we the consequences. The time has come for all of us to lay down our bets."

The werewolf howled loudly.

"And what happens if it doesn't work?" he barked.

"Then what must be will be," the pale, motionless corpse concluded. The two hobgoblins lowered the lid of his coffin, and with that the meeting came to a close.

At home the grown-ups were acting as if they all had for a long time secretly believed it best that we leave our home and travel to England, Scotland, or some other faraway place.

From out of nowhere an owl appeared in the dungeon. After circling the room once, she landed on our table and informed us that she had been sent with a message from the most powerful of all spirits.

Although the owl said nothing about what would happen if we didn't do what was requested of us by the man in the coffin, I had the feeling that it would be something pretty gruesome. Anyway, none of us would have thought to question the orders of such an influential spirit. Even I realized the seriousness of what was involved.

We knew what had to be done; all we needed was a plan.

We talked it over until dawn; then each of us lay in bed brooding about it during the day. In the evening the discussion began again at breakfast. Hundreds of suggestions were made, each one less promising than the one before.

"Stop this, stop it at once!" Grandfather pleaded. "I'm losing my head from all this talk."

"We need to succeed," Papa said stubbornly, because I think he felt the threat of punishment weighed most heavily on him. "We MUST MUST MUST!"

"Let's not deceive ourselves," Grandfather said. "I've said it a thousand times, and I'll say it again: Our time has passed. We've known it for a long time. We've only been pretending to frighten people because it was better not to try than to fail. We've been fooling each other and ourselves—living in the past with nothing more than ghosthood memories."

Naturally Grandmama wouldn't accept what Grandfather was saying. "We can think up new methods, think up new methods perhaps," she said. "We know that howling, blowing up, disappearing, and gnashing our teeth aren't enough anymore. We've learned that the hard way, we have."

"We can't possibly think of anything as frightening as the ways people have already thought up to frighten themselves," Grandfather stated. He told us that some-

times, when he was having a bit to drink in the tavern after human hours, he read their newspapers. "I once saw a headline that said, 'The Specter of Unemployment.' I have no idea what kind of specter that was supposed to be, but it's one the humans thought up themselves. And they seem to be truly afraid of it."

"You mean they don't need us anymore?" Lily asked.

"I've read," Grandfather continued, "that people have invented bombs and rockets that can destroy the world within minutes. You must understand: Everything that we can do to them is laughable compared to what they can do to themselves."

"But there must still be hope for us." Papa interrupted.

"The way they live has a great deal to do with why it has become so difficult for us to be effective," Grandfather continued. "In the past people used to gather together in the evenings. They told stories—sometimes even ghost and horror stories."

"Yes," Papa said. His face lit up with the memory of those times. "Yes, and if one hears enough about

ghosts, there's no telling what one begins to believe."

"But today," Grandfather went on, "they sit night after night in front of their televisions. They fear only the things they hear on television, and they talk about little else besides oil prices, housing costs, and money problems."

"They are so afraid of what they might do to each other," Grandfather said, "that they've forgotten how to be afraid of us. But instead of trying to figure out a way to solve their problems, they go on acting as if everything—"

Mama interrupted him. "We've heard enough about why people are no longer afraid of us. Where is all this talk getting us?"

"In your opinion," Papa said, "what would get us somewhere?"

"An idea," Mama answered. "I see that none of you has come up with one yet."

"Have you?" Papa asked.

"Could be," Mama said with a dangerous glint in her eyes. But she kept us in suspense, expecting us to

guess. "I thought so." She laughed finally. "Not even the simplest thing would occur to any of you."

"What is the simplest thing?" I asked.

"A child," was Mama's only answer.

"You mean, Max should scare a child?" Lily asked.

And Grandmama said in a low voice, "I don't know if that's fair; I don't know. A self-respecting ghost doesn't scare children."

"Oh, come on," Papa muttered. "In times like these you can't split bat hairs. You have to take what you can get."

"Max wouldn't have to scare a child to death," Mama said. "Just a little bit, enough to fulfill the wishes of the man in the coffin."

"Why didn't I think of that?" Papa wondered aloud. "A child. Of course, that's the solution! And that way I'll win my bet once and for all."

I . . . well, I agreed. I wasn't afraid of people anymore. What harm could there be in scaring a child with a little boo-ooo, I thought. But I decided it wouldn't be anything more than a small scare. *I still didn't un-*

derstand the reasons why spirits frightened humans, but the family honor was at stake. And I have to admit, I was even a little proud of the fact that the future of every ghost, ghoul, and spook depended on me.

Mama knew of a child who was said to be unusually timid.

The whole family wanted to take part in the event, but Mama wailed, "IMPOSSSSIBLE! Max and I are going alone. Imagine if by chance the child looks out of the window and sees an entire family of spooks . . . that would be too much. We can justify a boy ghost scaring a boy child, but anything else wouldn't look right."

So that night I again floated down to the village, this time with Mama.

She led me to a house and pointed up to a window on the second floor. "The boy I told you about lives here, and that's where he sleeps."

I only nodded. But after taking a deep breath, I floated upward. *Looking back on that moment today, I know that I did start out with everyone's best interests in mind. . . .*

The window, behind which the boy slept, was open a little. I looked down at Mama, who urged me on with a nod of encouragement, and slipped through the opening—into the room.

I couldn't see much of the little boy because he had the blankets pulled up to his ears. Silently I crept over to his bed. He seemed to be about as big as I was, which meant that he was about ten. (Human children, we learned in school, age ten times more quickly than ghost children.)

"Hello," I called softly. But the boy only turned onto his other side. "Hello, hello!" I tried again.

He finally opened his eyes. "Hmmm, what is it?" he asked. "Who's there?"

"I am," I said. "I'm a ghost. I'm supposed to scare you a little. But you really don't have any reason to be afraid of me. . . ."

Now the boy had become more alert. "My father says there's no such thing as ghosts," he said, although I noticed a tremor in his voice.

"Yes, there is!" I contradicted him. "We do exist.

But don't worry, I already told you I only want to scare you a little. I certainly don't want to give you a big fright. I think scaring people is silly. . . ."

The boy sat up. He reached for the lamp on his night table, but I stopped him; I wouldn't have been able to stand the bright light. In the meantime, his eyes had adjusted to the dark enough so that he could actually see me. "Yes, I th-think s-s-scaring people is s-s-silly, too-oo," he said. "And I-I-I'm r-r-really not a-a-fraid."

"Right," I said. "People are afraid only of what they don't know. But you're getting to know me, so you don't have to be afraid."

He looked at me with wide eyes and worked up the courage to ask, "A-A-Are you sure you're a real ghost? It's hard to believe because you don't look that frightening to me."

"Admit it, I scared you a little, didn't I?" I asked him.

"And how!" the boy said. "And for a second I was definitely afraid of you."

As far as I was concerned, I had accomplished what I had been sent to do.

"W-W-What do you want from me?" the boy asked.

"Oh, it's a long story," I said. "Let's just say that I wanted to pay you a visit. I've never been to a child's place, you know."

"And I've never b-b-been visited by a ghost before," the boy said. "It was a little creepy at first, but now that I'm getting used to you, it's kind of n-nice."

We sat beside each other on his bed for a while, and then I asked, "What should we do now?"

After thinking a moment, the boy cried, "I know!" He jumped up, tore the sheet off the bed (which sent me hovering), and put it over his head. In a deep voice he said, "Now I'm a ghossst, too! Boo-ooo!"

I had to laugh; he didn't look bad for a human. We jumped merrily around the room like two spooks at play.

We were laughing so loud and acting so crazy that

I didn't notice my mother had flown, like a bat, up to the window to watch my performance. When I turned and saw her, I knew she was ashamed of my behavior—she looked as if she wanted to vanish off the face of the earth.

I should have paid more attention to the low, thunderous growl that Mama sent forth from outside. But I didn't want to hear it. I was having so much fun playing with my new friend that I wasn't going to let anything interrupt us. The week before, I had been afraid of people, and there I was playing with a human child as if it were the most natural thing in the world. Secretly I even hoped that Mama, who was still fluttering outside the window, might consider that it was more fun to get along with people than to scare them. And perhaps, I thought, one night all ghosts will realize what we've been missing. . . .

We romped and jumped until we both were too tired to laugh. Then we sat down on the bed to catch our breaths.

Mama flew away from the window in a fury. But by

then I was convinced that I could show her how well humans and ghosts got along when they tried.

"What can we play now?" I asked the boy.

As if in answer, the windowpanes began to rattle and a terrible wind howled around the house, causing the entire structure to creak. "That doesn't mean anything," I said quickly when I saw the look of shock on my new friend's face. "That's only my mother raging a little."

But even as I said it, I knew I would never succeed in convincing Mama or any other grown-up spirit to make friends with humans. They were too pleased about being frightening, horrible, and intimidating to change their ways.

Then I remembered the assignment that had brought me to the house in the first place and the unspoken threat that accompanied it.

Suddenly I was as confused as I had been happy a few moments before.

The storm outside grew more threatening, and I feared that Mama would come inside if I stayed there with

the boy much longer. I couldn't let that happen; I couldn't
do that to my new friend.

"I think I have to go home now," I said. "It sounds
like a thunderstorm is coming."

"Does something happen to ghosts if they get wet?"
the boy asked.

I had to laugh. "Getting wet is the thing I'm least
afraid of."

"I'm afraid of thunder and lightning."

"You'll see," I said. "The storm will stop as soon as
I'm out the window."

"I wouldn't mind that," he said with a smile.

"I hope we'll see each other again."

"You can visit me anytime."

"I'll try," I said, hoping I'd be able to.

Then I gave myself a push and glided through the
window. WHAM! I felt myself hit, pounded, and
twisted—until I was so smashed up I could have fit
into a pickle jar.

It became clear to me that Mama *had* shut me up in
a pickle jar—to keep me from any other "IMPOSS-

SSIBLY silly acts"—only after I had been left that way, sitting high on a shelf back at the dungeon, for quite some time.

I tried to make as much noise as I could because I didn't think I could stand being in that cramped jar five minutes more. But no one was paying attention to me. The entire family was sitting around the table and appeared to be waiting for something. (Lily told me later just how terrible that period of waiting was.) Then, as if by magic, it appeared—a coffin stood in the dungeon, and two hobgoblins, neither of which anyone had seen come in, raised the lid. The werewolf arrived, and so did the man from the deep. Soon the room was filled with shadows darting here and there. Some of them even brushed against my pickle jar. Next, our neighbors Scream Bag and Babble Bag announced themselves. Uncle Dragul and Aunt Lilofee pushed their way in, and behind them,

all the teachers from the Ghost Academy. Papa's boss, the chief poltergeist, was there, as well as a whole crowd of ghosts and spirits whom I couldn't quite recognize because of the way I was squeezed into my pickle jar.

I couldn't understand what was being said or, rather, shouted, but their threatening gestures were made all the more dreadful in the bottled silence. I was so afraid that they would do something to my papa, my mama, or my grandparents out of anger because of what I had done, that I thought I'd explode.

To this day I have no idea how long that wild confrontation lasted. To be honest, it's still hard to think back on it.

Lily told me everyone agreed that my unghostly behavior had made the entire region of ghosts look ridiculous, had disgraced them once and for all. That left only two options open to us: emigration or retirement.

Looking back, I'm happy that I didn't have to listen to the whole thing. Lily maintains I stayed in the pickle jar for two whole weeks. It seemed to me like half an

eternity. Toward the end I lost interest in what was happening outside the jar. I think I dozed most of the time because it was so stuffy in there. At any rate, the first ghost I saw when they finally let me out was Uncle Percy, meaning that we were in England—or precisely the English earldom of Sussex.

We stayed there for only a few weeks, though, because soon after our arrival we received an offer from the Scottish highlands. And we've been here, at Loughnassie Castle, ever since.

The old castle is a hotel today. And the specialty of the house is ghosts—our family to be exact. The hotel brochure reads, "Spend a horrifying night in the haunted castle of Loughnassie!" People come from all over the British Isles to be part of the experience. They arrive with open minds and are determined not to leave without first being scared silly. Oh, well, as my grandfather always says, different countries, different customs.

Grandfather feels particularly at home here in Scotland. The castle's ghost and original owner, Sir James, has become his closest friend. Sir James, first duke of

Loughnassie, had the castle built eight hundred years ago. For some reason that he doesn't like to talk about, he was beheaded. Since that time he has wandered the halls with his head tucked under his arm. He and Grandfather often sit together in the tower, swapping stories. And sometimes if those two old gentleghosts have had one too many glasses of Scotch whisky, one of them wanders off with the wrong head.

Sir James constantly tells us how glad he is that we're helping out with the haunting. With the hotel's 140 beds, he used to rush around like a mad ghost in order to knock, rattle, and howl in each of the rooms between midnight and one o'clock. I'm not sure if people know that we can haunt the whole night through, not just during this "witching hour," but anyway, that's the time we're expected by the hotel guests.

"People are perfectly happy to pay for a good scare," Sir James says, "but they're not willing to lie awake all night."

Scotland

...Duke of Loughnassie

N E W S

Thurso

Loch Shin

Inverness

Ullapool

Dingwall

Loch Maree

Lewis

Skye

Draw a line from the swimmer's finger to the eye of the Loch Ness monster. Then draw a red cross halfway in between. That's where you'd find

Sir James...

148

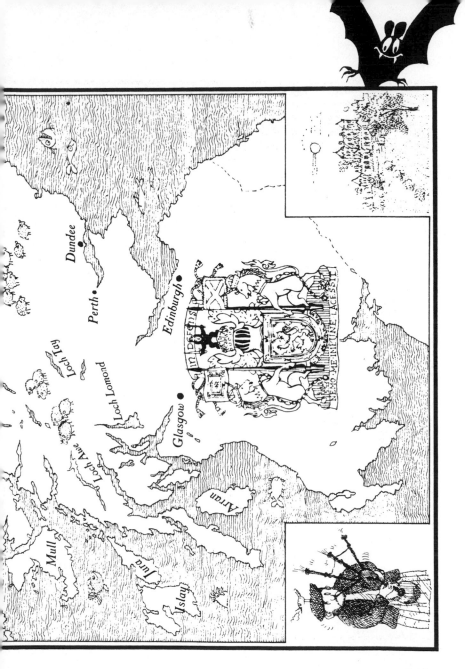

The hotel keeps our entire family busy—my parents, my grandparents, Lily, and even me. There are seven spooks in all, including Sir James, giving each of us twenty rooms to take care of. We all do our best to be considerate of the guests, and the hotel has a good reputation. It's known for the little extras it provides, such as especially long blankets on the beds, so guests can pull them over their heads if they get too frightened.

I guess you could say that everything worked out well. These days we rarely talk about what happened back home a year ago. And no one has criticized me for quite a while. The other spooks and spirits—who as it turns out, all left the homeland soon after we did—probably no longer hold a grudge. As Papa likes to remind us, "We hadn't had a future there for a long time."

Our relatives arrived safely in America. Aunt Lilofee wrote that Uncle Dragul took a FAAABULOUS job in Hollywood—consulting on vampire movies, if you can believe it!

Sometimes, when I'm floating over the Scottish moors after witching hour at the hotel, I still get a little homesick. But we'll be going on vacation soon, and the family has agreed it's time to go back to visit our old haunts.

Of course, no one knows that I'm planning to float by and see the boy I still call my friend.

I thought I might visit some other children, as well. You, for example, yes, you! I'd come only if you weren't afraid and if you wanted me to. So let me know. I'll be waiting to hear from you . . .

Don't worry about reaching me. I know you'll think of something.

151

Loughnassie Castle

* The original cornerstones of the castle built by Sir James.

Reader's Gallery

Suggestions:

> *Paste an old picture of yourself here ...*
> *or draw a self-portrait*
> *(you might even add vampire teeth).*
> *Write your name in ghostly lettering ...*
> *or make a greasy fingerprint.*
> *Think up your own way to make sure the*
> *spirits know about you ....*

This book belongs to:

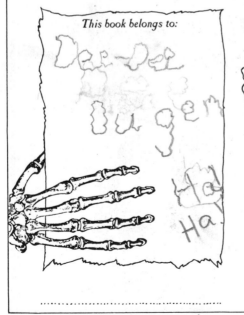

Which   I   Doo Doo Brain

Lindsay Duggan   Miles Duggan
                  and sarha
                  Primm

155

THE END

*with an appropriate
flutter
of wings!*